Bottoms Up

Skye Fargo slowly turned his head and stared into the muzzle of a revolver. Above it was Sharpton's florid face.

Wincing as he spoke, Sharpton snarled, "You didn't expect this, did you, you son of a bitch?"

Fargo decided to stall. "Care for a drink?"

Sharpton was stupefied. "I'm about to blow out your wick and you're offering me a drink?" He lowered his revolver a few inches. "What the hell kind of jackass are you?"

"Just to show there's no hard feelings for me hitting you," Fargo said.

"No hard . . . ?" Sharpton sputtered. "Mister, you damn near broke my jawbone. Hard feelings? Hell, yes, there are hard feelings." He lowered the barrel another inch or so. "You are one stupid bastard."

"One of us is," Fargo said, and exploded into motion. He whipped his left arm up and around, swatting the revolver aside, even as he smashed the bottle against the side of Sharpton's head . . .

THE

TRAILSMAN

#347

DAKOTA DEATH TRAP

by

Jon Sharpe

A SIGNET BOOK

SIGNET

Published by New American Library, a division of
Penguin Group (USA) Inc., 375 Hudson Street,
New York, New York 10014, USA
Penguin Group (Canada), 90 Eglinton Avenue East, Suite 700, Toronto,
Ontario M4P 2Y3, Canada (a division of Pearson Penguin Canada Inc.)
Penguin Books Ltd., 80 Strand, London WC2R 0RL, England
Penguin Ireland, 25 St. Stephen's Green, Dublin 2,
Ireland (a division of Penguin Books Ltd.)
Penguin Group (Australia), 250 Camberwell Road, Camberwell, Victoria 3124,
Australia (a division of Pearson Australia Group Pty. Ltd.)
Penguin Books India Pvt. Ltd., 11 Community Centre, Panchsheel Park,
New Delhi - 110 017, India
Penguin Group (NZ), 67 Apollo Drive, Rosedale, North Shore 0632,
New Zealand (a division of Pearson New Zealand Ltd.)
Penguin Books (South Africa) (Pty.) Ltd., 24 Sturdee Avenue,
Rosebank, Johannesburg 2196, South Africa

Penguin Books Ltd., Registered Offices:
80 Strand, London WC2R 0RL, England

First published by Signet, an imprint of New American Library,
a division of Penguin Group (USA) Inc.

First Printing, September 2010
10 9 8 7 6 5 4 3 2 1

The first chapter of this book previously appeared in *Arkansas Ambush*, the
three hundred forty-sixth volume in this series.

Copyright © Penguin Group (USA) Inc., 2010
All rights reserved

Ⓓ REGISTERED TRADEMARK — MARCA REGISTRADA

Printed in the United States of America

The Trailsman

Beginnings . . . they bend the tree and they mark the man. Skye Fargo was born when he was eighteen. Terror was his midwife, vengeance his first cry. Killing spawned Skye Fargo, ruthless, cold-blooded murder. Out of the acrid smoke of gunpowder still hanging in the air, he rose, cried out a promise never forgotten.

The Trailsman they began to call him all across the West: searcher, scout, hunter, the man who could see where others only looked, his skills for hire but not his soul, the man who lived each day to the fullest, yet trailed each tomorrow. Skye Fargo, the Trailsman, the seeker who could take the wildness of a land and the wanting of a woman and make them his own.

The Dakotas, 1861—The Trailsman is caught in a web of deceit.

1

The Sioux had been after Skye Fargo for five days.

A small fire was to blame. He had kindled it in a dry wash to roast a grouse. The evening sky had been clear, not a cloud in sight, which was why the gust of wind out of nowhere caught him by surprise. The next he knew, the flames leaped to a patch of grass and crackled to the top of the wash. He stomped most of the flames out and threw dirt on the rest but the harm had been done.

Fargo scanned the prairie and spotted riders on a low hill a quarter of a mile away. That they were warriors was obvious, and since he was in the heart of Sioux country, it wasn't hard to guess which tribe. He had a few friends among the Sioux; he had lived with a band once. But since of late the Sioux had been helping themselves to the hair of every white they came across, he'd rolled up his blankets and saddled the Ovaro and gotten the hell out of there.

No sooner did he burst out of the wash than war whoops rent the air and arrows buzzed like angry hornets. Fargo used his spurs and left the warriors breathing the stallion's dust. He'd figured that was the end of it. They couldn't track in the dark. He rode all night to be safe, only to discover, to his shock, that he wasn't. At first light there they were, half a mile back. One of them had to be a damn good tracker.

For five days Fargo pushed to the southeast. For five

days they doggedly stuck to his trail. He could have ambushed them. Find a spot and lie in wait and when they came in range, pick off as many as he could with his Henry. With a full tube and one in the chamber, the rifle held sixteen rounds. He was a marksman; he could drop half the war party before they collected their wits. But he kept on riding. He had made a pact with himself that he never killed unless he had to. Usually.

It was the middle of the morning on the sixth day when Fargo looked back and saw that the Sioux were no longer following him. They had turned around and were heading to the northwest, back into the heart of their territory. He drew rein and watched until they were out of sight. He wondered if it was a trick but he couldn't see how. He had too large a lead for them to circle around and lie in wait somewhere up ahead.

"I reckon they decided I wasn't worth the bother," Fargo summed up his thoughts out loud.

Before him rose green hills. He wound in among them and came on a stream. Climbing down at a shallow pool, he sank to a knee, dipped his hand in the water, and sipped. "Fit to drink," he announced, and let the stallion lower its muzzle.

Fargo could see his reflection. His buckskins were speckled with dust and his once white hat was practically brown. His red bandanna hung loose and could use retying. His blue eyes were a deeper blue than the water and his beard could use a trim. He went to dip his hand in again when the brush on the other side rustled and a horse snorted. Instantly, he swooped his right hand to his Colt. But he didn't draw.

Out of the brush came a woman tugging on the reins to a bay. Her back was to Fargo and she hadn't noticed him yet. All he saw was a black dress and a black shawl and a wealth of curly black hair. The bay was limping.

"Need some help there, ma'am?"

The woman spun. Fear froze her rigid and she blurted, "Oh! I didn't know you were there."

Now that Fargo could see the rest of her, he liked what he saw. She had lovely emerald eyes and full red lips that reminded him of ripe raspberries. Her dress was doing all it could to contain a pair of watermelons. And her legs, if the way the dress clung to them was any hint, went on forever. Unfurling, he smiled and said, "I didn't mean to startle you."

She looked back the way she had come. "They're still after me."

"Ma'am?"

"They're after me," she said again. "You'd best hide. I won't tell them I saw you."

"Who is after you?"

She turned. "Please," she said, her concern for his welfare genuine. "You don't know what they're like. They might think you're helping me and pistol-whip you. Or they might do it for the fun of it." She motioned up the stream. "Run while you still can."

Fargo gathered she was in some sort of trouble and some hard cases were after her. It was none of his affair, but then again, she was nice on the eyes. "I'm not going anywhere."

"You really must," the woman pleaded. "I don't want you hurt on my account."

Before Fargo could ask her to elaborate, the woods pealed to the drum of galloping hooves and five riders swept down on her. They were stamped from the same mold: hard-faced, cold-eyed men, wearing enough hardware for an armory. They were so intent on her that they didn't spot him until they came to a stop. A stocky block of flab in a short-brimmed brown hat with a tear in the brim thrust out a thick finger and bellowed.

"Who's that yonder?"

The woman had swung the bay so it was between her and the riders. She said, "You leave him be, Sharpton. I don't know him."

Sharpton had two chins and a bulbous nose. He wore a Beaumont-Adams revolver on his left side, butt forward for a cross draw. When he lowered his hand, he placed it on his belt an inch from the six-gun. "Who are you, mister?" he demanded. "And what the hell are you doing here?"

Fargo had been taking the measure of the others. Three were run of the mill frontier toughs. The last man, though, was different from the rest; he was tall—almost as tall as Fargo—and thin, and wore a black vest and a black hat and had a Smith and Wesson with walnut grips in a black leather holster high on his right hip. The man met Fargo's gaze, and nodded.

"Didn't you hear me?" Sharpton snapped.

"How could I not hear a big bag of wind like you?" Fargo answered, and stepped to the right so he was clear of the Ovaro.

"I asked you who you are," Sharpton said. "And I want to know what you're doing with this woman."

"I guess your pa never told you," Fargo said.

Sharpton blinked in confusion. "Eh?"

"That it's not smart to go around poking your big nose where it doesn't belong."

The rider in the black hat and vest chuckled.

"That's enough out of you, Blakely," Sharpton said.

"Oh?"

The man in the black hat and vest said it casually yet the effect it produced was instructive. The other three glanced at him and at Sharpton and reined their mounts to either side. As for Sharpton, his two chins bobbed and he quickly said, "I didn't mean nothing by that."

"Oh?" Blakely said again in that casual way of his.

"Damn it," Sharpton said. He had broken out in a sweat. "This is no time for you to be contrary. You want me to say I'm sorry? I'm sorry. Now can we get down to business and do what Mr. Mitchell told us to do?" He turned to the woman. "Mount up, Honeydew. We're to escort you a good long way and make sure you don't come back."

"Honeydew?" Fargo grinned.

"My last name. My first name is Jasmine."

Sharpton gigged his horse closer to hers. "I won't say it again. Get on. You're leaving and you're leaving now."

"What if I refuse?" Jasmine said.

"You're going anyway."

4

Fargo took another step. "No," he said. "She's not."

They looked at him, the five of them, four grimly serious. Blakely seemed more amused than anything. Sharpton glanced at the Colt in Fargo's holster and then stared at Fargo's face and uncertainty crept into his own.

"You don't want to buck us on this."

Fargo didn't respond.

"You have any idea who we work for, mister? Abe Mitchell."

"The handle means nothing to me."

"It should. He's got a small army of gun hands working for him and we all do as he says."

"Good for him."

Sharpton scowled and shifted in his saddle. "You're not getting my point. Bucking us is dumb. It could get you killed."

"You are welcome to try," Fargo said. "Or do you talk a man to death to get up the gumption?"

Blakely laughed.

As for Sharpton, he turned red in the face and his fingers clenched and unclenched. "You think I won't?"

"I think you're a yellow streak who only tries when he has an edge," Fargo said. "Now either jerk that smoke-wagon or get the hell out of here before I lose my temper."

Sharpton hauled on his reins and wheeled his mount. Glaring over his shoulder, he snarled, "This ain't over. We'll meet again. The only reason I don't do it now is that we're not to shoot anyone without Mr. Mitchell's say-so."

"Whatever excuse helps you sleep," Fargo said.

Sharpton used his spurs and the rest did the same except for Blakely who touched his hat brim to Honeydew and grinned at Fargo. "I should pay you for the entertainment. Watch your back if you drift into Hapgood Pond." He lifted the reins to go.

"Why are you riding with trash like Sharpton?" Fargo asked.

Blakely paused. "I thank you for the compliment." He sighed and gazed after the departing riders. "I have

5

no control over who else Mr. Mitchell hires to protect him."

"So it's just the money."

"A man does what he has to to put food in his belly." Again Blakely lifted the reins.

"You don't mind the sour taste in your mouth?"

Blakely's features hardened slightly. "You're dangerous, friend. I hope it doesn't come down to you and me. I'd hate to have to kill someone with your fine sense of humor." He nodded at Jasmine and calmly rode off at a walk.

"A strange man," Jasmine said quietly.

Fargo turned to her.

"He rides with those gun sharks but he's nothing like them," Jasmine said. "He's always polite to women, for one thing. And he talks better, for another. Yet they say he's the deadliest of all of them. They say he's so fast, you don't see his hand move when he draws."

"That's fast." Fargo could recall more than a few instances when the same had been said about him. "But let's talk about you." He gave her his most charming smile and ran his eyes from her lustrous hair to the tips of her small shoes. "God was nice to me today."

"You have hungry eyes, sir," Jasmine said.

"I haven't been with a woman in over a week."

"That long?" Jasmine smirked. "But you're right. God has been nice to both of us. More so than you can imagine." With that, she reached up and removed her shawl. Her dress was topped by a white collar that went completely around her neck.

"What the hell?" Fargo said. The last time he had seen a collar like that had been on a parson.

"I didn't fully introduce myself. I am *Reverend* Honeydew, a duly ordained minister. And I am pleased to meet you, my brother." She came over and held out her hand for him to shake.

"Brother?" Fargo repeated.

"We are all brothers and sisters in the eyes of the Lord."

"Son of a bitch," Fargo said.

"Now, now. I'll thank you not to curse in my presence, if you don't mind." Jasmine replaced her shawl and smoothed her dress, her watermelons jiggling with every movement.

Fargo sighed and turned to the Ovaro and gripped the saddle horn. "Be seeing you, ma'am."

"Hold on. Where are you going?"

"I'm heading east. I have to meet a man in Saint Louis at the end of the month about guiding a wagon train." Fargo went to hike his leg.

"No. Please. You can't leave."

"Why not?" Fargo had done his good deed for the year and had no hankering to stick around. She was an eyeful but getting her out of that dress would take more time and effort than he had to spare.

"You're an answer to my prayers."

"You're loco." Once more Fargo raised his boot.

"Please. Hear me out." Jasmine clasped her hands to her more than ample bosom. "Hapgood Pond is dearly in need of a shepherd. There are saloons and fallen doves. And where you have drink and tarts you have sinners."

Fargo thought of all the doves he had been with but kept it to himself.

"For some reason Abe Mitchell doesn't like outsiders," Jasmine had gone on. "I was told that his men have run a number of travelers off. Sharpton was doing the same to me when I stumbled on you."

"What the hell harm can a preacher do?"

"I think Sharpton got carried away. I hadn't been in Hapgood Pond an hour when he showed up and began badgering me with questions. When I didn't answer to his satisfaction, he pushed me and told me to get out. He said that if I didn't, he would do things to me." She stopped and blushed. "You can imagine what kind of things. Anyway, he marched me to my horse and made me ride off. I yelled at him that I would be back, and that's when he and the others came after me."

"Running off strangers is peculiar."

"Isn't it though? So there I was, in desperate straits,

7

and out of the blue you showed up. Do you see what that means?"

"I am a flame and good-looking women are the moths."

"What? No. Why would you say a thing like that?" Jasmine shook her head. "This was divine design. God sent you to help me."

"Oh, hell," Fargo said.

"Return with me to Hapgood Pond and see that I am not run off a second time."

Fargo thought of the saloons and the doves, especially the doves. "Preacher lady, lead the way."

2

Hapgood Pond was a new settlement. It boasted a general store and a feed and grain and a butcher shop that doubled as the barber shop; the man who owned it chopped meat and hair, both. There were two saloons plus a number of cabins and frame houses. Since people couldn't live without water, most settlements were built near rivers or streams or lakes. This one was the first Fargo came across that was built near a pond. It covered about three acres. On the south shore stood an old cabin all by itself.

Fargo was aware of the eyes on him as he dismounted and tied the Ovaro to the hitch rail in front of the general store. Pale faces peered from many of the windows. "Folks don't have a lot to do around here, do they?"

Reverend Jasmine Honeydew was still on her horse, sitting straight and proud and looked around as if defying anyone to object to her being there. "They will once I set them to work building my church."

"Maybe they won't want one."

"Every community needs a house of worship," Jasmine said. "I'll appeal to their better natures."

"What if they don't have any?"

"Are you suggesting that they *like* living in sin and depravity? It might seem to be a peaceful little hamlet at the moment but you haven't seen Hapgood Pond at night. It turns into Sodom and Gomorrah, only worse."

9

"No place is as bad as you make this one out to be," Fargo told her. Truth was, he liked lively night life as much as he liked anything. "Now if you'll excuse me." He headed for the nearest whiskey mill. A crude sign said it was the Blue Heron. A strange name for a saloon, he thought, until he glanced toward the pond and saw a blue heron.

"Where are you going? You can't just up and leave. What if Abe Mitchell or his men give me trouble?"

Fargo turned. "I came for a drink and a game of cards and if I am lucky, one of those fallen doves you mentioned will take a shine to me." He went to the batwings and pushed on in. It wasn't noon yet and the place was practically deserted. The bartender was sweeping the floor. Over in a corner an old man was sucking on a bottle that appeared to be empty, and at a table in the middle of the room sat a plump brunette in a tight red dress playing solitaire. They all looked at him as he crossed to the bar.

"Be right with you," the bartender said.

The dove had a nice smile and man-hungry eyes. "Hello, there, handsome. Care to buy a lady a drink?"

"In a minute," Fargo said. He paid for a bottle and the bartender placed two glasses next to it. Scooping them up, Fargo turned and nearly collided with the old man, who grinned a next-to-toothless grin. "What the hell?"

"Sorry, young fella. But I was wondering if you'd care to buy an old coon like me a drink, too? I ain't as pretty as Maude but I am right friendly."

Fargo's nose tingled with an odor that was part sweat and part whiskey and part worse. Before he could reply the bartender smacked the counter and snapped, "Damn it, Hapgood. What have I told you about bothering my customers?"

"I can't help being thirsty."

"Hapgood?" Fargo said. "You the gent they named this place after?"

"That would be me. Charley Hapgood, at your service." Hapgood did his best imitation of a courtly bow. "That's my cabin over by the pond. I was the first here and the only one until some farmers came along and then Webster with his general store and Herbert with his feed and grain and now Abe Mitchell and his gun crowd."

"The gent who doesn't like strangers," Fargo said.

"He's a strange one, that's for sure."

"His men won't like you talking about him," the bartender said.

"I ain't afeared of them, Milo. They wouldn't waste the lead on an old cuss like me." Hapgood fixed rheumy eyes on Fargo. "What do you say to that bug juice, mister?"

"I won't have you begging for drinks," Milo declared, and started to reach across the bar.

"No," Fargo said. He set the glasses down, filled one, and held it out.

Charley Hapgood took it in trembling fingers and delicately raised it to his mouth as if afraid to spill a single drop. He sipped and closed his eyes and smiled in delight.

"I thank you, young fella. If I can ever do you a favor, you let me know."

Both spindly hands wrapped around the glass, Charley Hapgood shuffled toward the corner table.

"Sorry about him, mister," Milo said, sliding another glass across. "He pesters everybody. The other saloon won't let him set foot inside, he's such a nuisance."

"You let him."

Milo shrugged. "I sort of feel sorry for the old buzzard. He doesn't have many years left."

The dove was placing a red six on a red seven when Fargo hooked a chair with his boot, pulled it out, and sat. "Maude, is it? I see you cheat."

"A girl does what she has to to get ahead." Maude grinned and accepted a glass and studied him as he poured. "You probably hear this a lot but you are one handsome son of a bitch."

Fargo dispensed with a glass and chugged straight from the bottle. After more than a week without, the whiskey was a treat. He drank about a third and set the bottle down and belched.

11

"I take it your ma didn't learn you any manners?" Maude teased.

"She taught me to take my spurs off before I climb into bed."

"Ah. Just so you learned the important things." Chortling, Maude upended her glass and drained it in a gulp.

"Damn," Fargo said.

Maude waggled her glass. "Don't be stingy, handsome. Get me lubricated and you are in for a night you won't forget."

"I'll keep that in mind." Fargo refilled her glass and leaned on his elbows. "Tell me something. You're not worried, with this settlement so close to Sioux territory?"

"Hell. Why'd you go and ask a thing like that?" Maude downed her second glass in two swallows instead of one. "Like you say, we're not *in* their territory—we're near it. They've left us be so far and I hope it stays that way." She sniggered. "Besides, another five years and Hapgood Pond will be a regular town with a hundred farms and ranches everywhere and an army post nearby. Those damned redskins won't dare lift a finger against us."

"Where did you hear all that?" Fargo often scouted for the army and this was the first he had heard of a new post.

"Some of Mitchell's men were talking like there would be one." Maude looked at him intently. "Say. I just realized. You must be another of his hired guns. Did you just sign on?"

"No and no," Fargo said. "I'm passing through." He sat back and swigged and heard a commotion outside, a few loud voices and rough laughter. He thought nothing of it.

"That's a shame. The rest of the girls get a gander at you, they'll be drawing lots to see who gets to rip your britches off."

Fargo laughed. "Hell, they can take turns."

"Listen to you. A buck in rut."

The voices grew louder. Fargo heard the words "lady

preacher" and "try it and you'll like it" and more gruff mirth. "Be right back," he said to Maude.

Over in front of the general store Sharpton and two of the curly wolves who had been with him earlier were having fun at Reverend Jasmine Honeydew's expense. Sharpton had a whiskey bottle and was trying to force her to take a drink. The other two had hold of her arms. She was standing tall and straight with her mouth clamped shut and each time Sharpton shoved the bottle at her, she turned her head.

"Idiots everywhere," Fargo said. He drew his Colt as he came up on them. They were so focused on having their fun with her that they didn't hear him.

Sharpton grabbed hold of the back of the minister's head to keep her from moving and shoved the bottle against her lips. "You're going to drink, damn it. Then you're leaving Hapgood Pond and not coming back."

"Can I have some?" Fargo asked.

Sharpton spun in surprise. "You!" he exclaimed.

"Me," Fargo said, and slammed the Colt's barrel against the man's jaw. Sometimes it took two or three blows but with Sharpton it took only one; his knees buckled and down he crashed. The pair holding the reverend were rooted in surprise. Pointing the Colt, Fargo warned them, "I'll only say this once. Let go of the lady."

They acted as if she was on fire.

"Now pick up your peckerwood of a pard and haul him back to whatever hole you crawled out of." Fargo covered them as they gripped Sharpton's arms and dragged him to their mounts in front of the butcher shop. They threw Sharpton over his saddle, none too gently, and quickly climbed on their mounts and reined out of the settlement to the south.

"Thank you," Reverend Honeydew said.

Fargo twirled the Colt into his holster and made it to the batwings before she caught up with him.

"Didn't you hear me?"

"Just fine." Fargo tried to enter but she held on to his elbow.

13

"They were going to get me drunk so I would go with them quietly."

"I gathered as much." Fargo smiled and tapped his hat and was halfway inside when she grabbed him again.

"Wait. Please. Have you thought it over? Being my protector, I mean? I'll pay you for your services." She undid her shawl so that the white collar showed. "I don't have a lot but I can afford, say, a dollar a week."

"You expect me to maybe have my head busted or take lead for less than fifteen cents a days?" Fargo snorted and shrugged her hand off and went in. He figured that was the end of it but the batwings creaked and she was at his side, wringing her hands.

"I'm asking nicely."

"Go away."

"What if I beg?"

"Some reverend you are." Fargo plopped into his chair and let the whiskey sear his throat. When he lowered the bottle she was still there. "You are becoming a nuisance."

Maude was gaping at the minister in wide-eyed wonderment. "Pardon me, ma'am. Does that collar mean what I think it does?"

Fargo did the honors. "Reverend Honeydew, meet Maude. Maude, meet Reverend Pain In The Ass."

"Oh my," Maude said. "A real life female preacher. I didn't know they had such a thing."

"Oh, yes, my dear," Jasmine said. "The Congregational Church has been ordaining women for ten years or better. I am one of a score of female preachers of the gospel."

"My word!" Maude said in amazement.

Fargo drank more whiskey.

"I've come to this settlement to shed light in the darkness and bring sinners to repentance."

"You don't say." Maude was enthralled.

Just then Milo called out from behind the bar, "Are you here to ask for work, lady? I can use another pair of tits and legs but you supply your own dress and I get half of what you make."

14

Jasmine Honeydew turned and put a hand to her white collar. "I beg your pardon?"

"God Almighty! Is that for real?" Milo glanced at Fargo, who nodded and swallowed more whiskey. "Well, look, ma'am or reverend or whatever I should call you. People will get the wrong idea, you being in here. A watering hole is no place for a fine woman like yourself."

"Thanks, Milo, you bastard," Maude said.

"Are you throwing me out?" Reverend Honeydew asked.

"No, ma'am. I'm asking nice and polite for you to take your Bible pushing somewhere else."

Jasmine looked at Fargo. "Do you see what I am up against? Now do I have your help or don't I?"

"You don't."

"What must I do to persuade you? Get down on my knees? Very well."

To Fargo's consternation she proceeded to kneel and pressed her hands together and raised them to him.

"I'm begging you."

"Oh my," Maude said.

Milo came hustling around the end of the bar. "What in the world are you doing, lady? This ain't no church. Get out of here before you scare my customers off."

"I implore you," Jasmine said to Fargo. "You have stood up for me twice. All I'm asking is that you go on standing up for me when the need requires. With your help I can convert the sinners here in no time."

"Do what?" Milo said.

"Isn't she wonderful?" Maude declared.

"Hell." Fargo didn't want any part of this silliness. Any other female pestered him as she was doing, he would turn them around and plant his boot on their backside. But that wouldn't do for a woman of the cloth. Not with witnesses.

"Listen to me, Reverend. I'm not here to hold your hand. I came to drink and play cards and get laid."

Maude put her hand to her throat in dismay. "Shame on you. You shouldn't talk to a minister that way."

"Forgive him, sister," Reverend Honeydew said. "He knows not what he does."

"Hell in a basket." Fargo grabbed his bottle and stomped to the batwings and out into the glare of the afternoon sun. He made it a point to swing the batwings behind him so that if Reverend Honeydew came after him it might knock her on her ass. No such luck. When he glanced back she was huddled with the dove and they were talking as if they were long-lost sisters. "Women!" he grumbled, and took a swallow.

The street, such as it was, was deserted save for horses at several of the hitch rails and a pig that was rubbing itself against a post.

Fargo jammed his hat brim low over his eyes and walked toward the pond. At least there he could drink in peace. A boulder proved handy and he sat and sipped and watched a pair of mallards. A fish jumped, and somewhere a frog croaked. He was raising the bottle when he heard something else.

Behind him, a gun hammer clicked.

3

Skye Fargo slowly turned his head and stared into the muzzle of a Beaumont-Adams revolver. Above it was Sharpton's florid face. The lower half was swollen and the skin along the jaw discolored.

Wincing as he spoke, Sharpton snarled, "You didn't expect this, did you, you son of a bitch?"

No, Fargo hadn't, and he should have. He was about to have his brain cored for being careless. He decided to stall. "Care for a drink?"

"What?"

Fargo hefted the bottle. "It's Crescent," he said, referring to the brand. "Burns like hell going down."

Sharpton was stupefied. "I'm about to blow out your wick and you're offering me a drink?" He lowered his revolver a few inches. "What the hell kind of jackass are you?"

"Just to show there's no hard feelings for me hitting you," Fargo said.

"No hard . . . ?" Sharpton sputtered. "Mister, you damn near broke my jawbone. Hard feelings? Hell, yes, there are hard feelings." He lowered the barrel another inch or so. "You are one stupid bastard."

"One of us is," Fargo said, and exploded into motion. He whipped his left arm up and around, swatting the revolver aside, even as he smashed the bottle against the side of Sharpton's head, knocking Sharpton's hat off.

The bottle shattered, spraying whiskey and glass shards. Sharpton staggered—but didn't go down. Blood flowing from a gash above his ear, he bellowed in rage and thrust his revolver at Fargo's face. Fargo grabbed Sharpton's wrist and drove his fist into the gunman's gut. Sharpton grunted, twisted, and with surprising strength shoved Fargo toward the ground. Only Fargo's grip on Sharpton's wrist kept him on his feet. He punched Sharpton again, in the head. It was like punching an anvil. Suddenly Sharpton flung out a boot, tripping him. Fargo tottered into the pond. He tried to regain his balance but Sharpton pushed again and down he went. He pulled the gunman after him and wound up on his back with Sharpton on his chest.

"I'm going to drown you!"

The water was only a few inches deep. It came as high as Fargo's ear. He bucked and nearly threw Sharpton off. He bucked a second time, and was jolted by a knee to the stomach that whooshed the breath from his body and momentarily left him weak. Instantly, Sharpton half rose and hauled him toward deeper water.

"I've got you now!"

Fargo had other ideas. One knee deserved another; he drove his into Sharpton's groin. The gunman gurgled and doubled over, his face a purple beet. Heaving upward, Fargo got to his knees. If he could draw his Colt he could finish it in a heartbeat but he didn't dare let go of Sharpton's wrist or he would be shot. He tried to rise higher but Sharpton butted him in the forehead and fireflies swirled.

Lunging upward, he drove his head against Sharpton's jaw. It caused more fireflies but it also caused Sharpton to take a step back. Wrenching his arm free, Fargo smashed his fist against the gunman's chin.

The gunman swayed.

Fargo hit him again and Sharpton arced a fist at his face. Fargo jerked his head aside. Girding his legs, he launched himself like a battering ram. His shoulder caught Sharpton across the middle and knocked him back. Fingers clawed at his eyes. He slugged the gunman twice more. Then dry ground was under them and he let loose with an uppercut that rocked Sharpton onto his boot heels. Leaping straight up, Fargo slammed his knee against Sharpton's elbow. Sharpton yelped and dropped the Beaumont-Adams.

Fargo waded in. He delivered a right to the jaw, a left cross to the neck, a right to the cheek that opened it like a split melon, another left, and finally another uppercut that lifted the gunman clear off the ground and sent him crashing to earth, unconscious.

Breathing heavily, Fargo stood over Sharpton, his fists still clenched. The smart thing to do was to kill him. He put his hand on his Colt.

"You wouldn't!"

Fargo looked up.

Reverend Jasmine Honeydew was aghast. "You wouldn't shoot a defenseless human being?"

"He was about to shoot me."

"I know. I saw the whole thing."

"You saw him come up behind me and didn't warn me?" Fargo had half a mind to slug *her* but he didn't hit women unless they were trying to do him harm.

"I was about to and then I saw you two were talking, so I came over to ask him to put his six-shooter away." She motioned at the sprawled bloody form. "Then this happened."

Fargo knew he would regret it but he took his hand off the Colt. "You are a trial, woman."

"What did I do?"

Fargo shook his head. He picked up the Beaumont-Adams, turned, and threw it. It disappeared under the water with a *plop*. One of his knuckles was scraped raw and bleeding. He licked the blood off and moved past her toward the Blue Heron. Maude, Milo the bartender, and Charley Hapgood were at the front window. He glared at them and went to the bar and around it to the long shelf.

"Here now," Milo said. "What are you doing?"

Fargo helped himself to another bottle, slapped coins on the bar, and took a long chug. He saw the lady minister staring at him over the batwings and ignored her. Striding to the window, he took hold of Maude's hand. "Where's your room?"

"Now?" Maude said.

"It's five dollars a poke," Milo brought up.

"Where?" Fargo growled.

Maude nervously led him toward a hall at the back. "This way, handsome. I don't usually do this so early in the day but with you I'll make an exception." She jiggled her wide bottom.

Just before he went down the hall Fargo glanced over his shoulder at Reverend Jasmine Honeydew, and grinned. She blushed and walked off.

"That fight made you randy, did it?" Maude prattled. "It happens sometimes. We get drunks fighting all the time. Some need a woman, after, to calm themselves."

Fargo lubricated his throat.

"Milo is a stickler for the five dollars or I'd do you for free. But if he doesn't get the money the boss will have him whipped."

Fargo couldn't care less but he asked, "Milo doesn't own the saloon?"

"Goodness, no. He just works here. Abe Mitchell owns the Blue Heron. Once a month like clockwork he rides in and helps himself to a dozen bottles and takes them back to his house." Maude came to a door and opened it. Inside was a small bedroom with a small rug and a table and chair. The bed had brass rails at the top and bottom. There was no window. She giggled and lit a lamp, then closed the door. "This here is my bedwor, as those fancy French folks say."

Fargo knew the right word but he didn't correct her. He upended the bottle, then asked, "Mitchell ever pay you for a poke?"

"No. He never shows any interest in me or any of the other girls. But what are we talking about him for when you have something better on your mind?" She cupped her breasts and grinned. "I am yours to command."

Fargo set the bottle on the table. He hung his hat on

a peg and undid his gun belt and placed it next to the bottle.

Maude giggled lustfully. "Wait until the other girls hear what they missed. That's what they get for sleeping in. Most don't get up until the middle of the afternoon. Me, I'm always up with the chickens. Comes from being born on a farm, I reckon."

"You talk too much."

"Be nice. I don't ask a lot of the men I let poke me but I do ask them to be nice."

"I'll be nice to these," Fargo said, and replaced her hands with his own.

Maude gasped as if it came as a surprise and her mouth puckered in invite. "You don't beat around the bush, do you?"

"I'm not paying five dollars for gab."

Fargo hungrily covered her mouth with his. Her tongue made little darting thrusts and he sucked on it and she moaned. Her nipples were like tacks. He pinched them through her dress and she moaned louder. Suddenly her hands were everywhere, caressing, exploring. He eased her toward the bed and she sank onto her back with the ease of long practice. She eagerly pried and plucked at his buckskin pants. When his member sprang free, she looked at it with hooded lids and ran her fingers its entire length.

"My, oh my. What have we here?"

"Don't act as if you've never seen one."

"Oh, I've seen plenty," Maude said. "I've just never seen many as fine as yours."

To shut her up Fargo kissed her and went on kissing her as he undid buttons and stays to get at her charms. It took some doing. He figured it must take her half an hour to put on her dress in the morning because it took him half that long to shed it. Or so it seemed. Her cotton chemise was next. For their size, her breasts were firm. They were also sensitive. A single lick of his tongue between her cleavage and she ground herself against him and cooed. Meanwhile, her fingers were busy on his pole. She knew just what to do. In no time he was fit to explode but he held off.

Fargo ran his hand over the convex swell of her belly to her bushy thatch. He slid his palm down her soft-as-silk thigh to her knee and back again. Her skin was warm to his touch. He pressed a finger to her moist slit and her body rippled with pleasure he provoked.

"I want you in me, handsome. I want you in me now."

Positioning himself on his knees, Fargo spread her legs. She pushed his hands off his member and replaced them with her own. A lift of her hips and the deed was done; his throbbing organ was imbedded in her velvet sheath. She moved her bottom provocatively. He matched her rhythm, prepared to last a good long while.

"Yes!" Maude exclaimed. "Make me spurt, handsome."

Fargo slid a hand between them and flicked her tiny knob. It nearly brought her up off the bed. She kissed him with fierce passion, then suddenly pumped with wild abandon. Sensing her need for release, he drove harder into her.

At his third stroke she clutched his shoulders and stifled a scream. Her nails drew blood from his shoulders. The bed creaked and thumped, the brass rails squeaking like a legion of mice.

"Now!" Maude said. "Now!"

Fargo didn't need to ask what she meant. She burst like a dam, an inner flood that for some reason made him think of the reverend. He inhaled a nipple and nipped it with his teeth. Maude cried out, thrashed wildly, and gradually coasted to a stop. Limp and spent, she smiled dreamily.

"That was a switch. Usually it is me who makes them spurt. You are something special, mister."

"I'm not done."

"What?"

Fargo gripped her hips and rammed up into her. "My turn." He commenced to rock on his knees, burying himself to the hilt again and again and again. Maude closed her eyes and clung to him as if she was drowning and he was a log. Tiny mews fluttered from her throat, growing louder the longer Fargo took.

He orchestrated his movements to mesh with hers. Her urgency built. She panted in his ear, saying, "Yes, yes, yes, yes, yes."

Their release nearly broke the bed. They were pounding so fiercely that the brass rail at the top snapped and from under them came the *twang* of a busted spring. Fargo rammed and rammed until he was drained and then he collapsed on top of her, her melons cushioning his cheek. She quaked for a good two minutes, her whole body awash in the ecstasy of the aftermath. At last she subsided and lay still.

"Damn, that was fine."

Fargo rolled onto his side and draped his arm across her. His eyelids were leaden.

"Are you married?"

"Hush."

"I was just asking." Maude pecked him on the cheek and on the neck and reached down and cupped him.

"Too soon for a second helping," Fargo sleepily informed her.

"I want to remember it."

"Draw it on paper, why don't you?"

Maude tittered and ran her fingers along his manhood and pulled at the tip. "I wish I could chop this off and keep it in a sack and use it whenever I wanted."

Cracking an eye, Fargo regarded her as he might a rabid wolf. "Where I go, it goes."

"I was only saying."

"And I'd like to cut off your tits and make saddlebags out of them," Fargo rejoined.

"You're just being silly."

Fargo closed his eyes to try and get some sleep and the next moment someone knocked on the door.

"Is that you, Milo?" Maude hollered.

"It's Reverend Honeydew."

"Oh God," Maude said.

"I need to talk to Mr. Fargo."

"Tell her to go jump off a cliff," Fargo said to Maude, who chortled and raised her head.

"I'm sorry, but he doesn't want to talk to you right now."

"It's important."

"Maybe you should come back later," Maude advised.

"Very well," the minister said. "I just thought Mr. Fargo would want to know about his horse. He seemed quite fond of it."

Despite himself, Fargo rose on an elbow. "What about my horse, Reverend?"

"Mr. Sharpton is stealing it."

4

Fargo didn't bother strapping on his gun belt. He yanked the Colt from the holster, threw the door wide, and shouldered past a startled Jasmine, who glanced down and blushed. He hitched at his pants as he ran. Milo and Charley Hapgood were at the front window, looking out. They heard him and turned, and Milo said, "You're too late."

Fargo burst out the batwings and into the street. Honeydew's horse was still tied to the hitch rail in front of the general store but the Ovaro was gone. He glanced up and down the street and then barreled back into the Blue Heron. "Sharpton took it?"

Charley Hapgood nodded. "Yes, sir, he did. The reverend told us and ran back to fetch you. We looked out and saw that Sharpton fella riding off and leading your animal by the reins."

"He was laughing," Milo said.

"Where would he go with it?" Fargo asked, barely able to control his fury. On the frontier stealing a man's horse was a lynching offense.

"Abe Mitchell's, most likely."

"Where is that?"

"Mitchell has a house about half a mile out to the east. Follow the road, such as it is. You can't miss it."

Fargo stalked toward the back hall. There were some things he wouldn't abide, ever, and this was at the top of the list.

25

Reverend Honeydew had her hands primly folded in front of her. "He said to give you a message."

"Sharpton?"

"I was in the store buying a few things. When I came out he was on his horse and had hold of yours. His face looked awful, all puffy and black and blue, with dry blood everywhere."

"He's going to bleed a lot more," Fargo vowed.

"I asked him what he thought he was doing and he said to give you a message. He said that he wanted to make sure you didn't leave before he got back so he was taking your horse."

"He's coming back?"

"With friends. Abe Mitchell has over a dozen gun hands working for him. I imagine they will want words with you."

"Words, my ass." Fargo strode past her.

Maude was putting herself together and jumped when he stomped into her bedroom. "Was it true what she told us?"

Fargo nodded as he strapped on his gun belt.

"Sharpton never was very bright. I wouldn't want to be in his boots when you catch up to him."

Fargo sat on the bed and tugged on his boots. First he made sure the ankle sheath that held his Arkansas toothpick was good and tight. Counting out five dollars, he placed the money on the table. "This is for the frolic."

"You are most welcome, kind sir," Maude said in her exaggerated fashion. "Feel free to visit my bedwor any time."

"You're a hoot, Maude," Fargo said. He took his bottle and went out. It took several swallows to calm him enough that he could think straight.

Milo was staring at him as if he expected to be shot.

"I hear tell Mitchell owns this place," Fargo mentioned.

"That he does. Word is, he had it built just so he would have someplace to drink."

"Big fish in a small pond," Fargo said.

Charley Hapgood had come over holding an empty glass. "Don't insult my pond, mister. It's not the biggest but it ain't puny, either."

"You said you were here first?"

"Sure was. I don't like people much so I came way out here to be by myself. Then a few farmers drifted in. The stores were built and houses went up and here I am, up to my neck in two-legged critters."

"I am no critter," Milo said.

Fargo was puzzled. "Why here of all places?" He could think of a score of better spots for people to settle. Hell, there were hundreds of miles of good river land along the Platte and other waterways just waiting to be claimed.

"Beats me," Charley said. "Maybe they liked my pond as much as I do. Those ducks are awful cute."

"You are missing a few bales," Milo said.

"It was Abe Mitchell who named the place," Charley imparted. "Came in one day and I went up to him and said as how I didn't like having people all over and why couldn't he and everyone else pack up and leave? Damned if he didn't pat me on the head like I was an infant and said that to make it up to me, from now on the settlement would be named after me."

Fargo refilled Hapgood's glass. "For the information, old-timer."

"Hell, it was free," Charley said. He grinned and eagerly took a sip. "Damn me if whiskey ain't the best thing ever invented. It almost makes it bearable."

"Makes what bearable?" Milo asked.

"Living," Charley said.

"Any more of Mitchell's men in the settlement right this minute?" Fargo wanted to know.

Charley took another loud sip. "There's two over to the Sagebrush. Saw them go in right before your horse was took. I expect they're still there."

"I'm obliged." Fargo walked out and was once again aware of faces at the windows. The people had nothing better to do except watch what everyone else was doing.

The Sagebrush Saloon was smaller than the Blue Heron. A rail-thin barkeep was stacking glasses. At a table were two men with a bottle of rye between them. They were sitting there talking and didn't pay much attention to Fargo until he walked up to the table and said, "Shed your hardware."

The pair looked at him and then at one another and at him again. One wore a flannel shirt and a straw skimmer, of all things, and had a revolver on his left side. The other was younger and had a brown hat and a brown vest and a Volcanic pistol with pearl grips. He was the one who replied, "What was that, mister?"

"Take off your gun belts and put them on the table."

"Why in hell would we do that?" Straw Skimmer wanted to know.

"Because you're leaving Hapgood Pond."

They swapped confused glances and the man with the Volcanic said, "Are you loco? We're not going anywhere. But maybe you are. Our boss doesn't like strangers."

"The gun belts," Fargo insisted. It would be two less he might have to go up against later. Better to cut the odds now, he reckoned, than wait for Sharpton to come at him with a small army.

"Are you drunk?" Straw Skimmer asked.

"He must be," Volcanic said. "Waltzing in here and bossing us around." He fixed a hard stare on Fargo. "We don't work for you. We work for Abe Mitchell. Only Mr. Mitchell gets to tell us what to do."

"That's where you're wrong." Fargo shifted his right hand so it brushed his holster.

At a nod from Volcanic the pair pushed their chairs back and stood. Straw Skimmer appeared unsure but not Volcanic. He stepped away from the table and lowered his hand close to his holster.

"Mister, you have a lot of gall. I will count to five and by then you better be gone."

Fargo had nothing against these men. If he were one of them, he would be as angry as they were. But he had it to do, and he made a last try to avert bloodshed.

"Does Mitchell pay you enough to take lead for him?"

"He hired us to help protect him," Volcanic said.

Fargo's curiosity got the better of him. "Who would be out to get him way out here?"

"Maybe you," Volcanic said.

Fargo thought of the Ovaro. "None of that gives his men the right to steal a horse."

"What the hell are you talking about?"

"Sharpton just stole mine."

"The hell you say," Straw Skimmer said.

"Why?" Volcanic asked.

"We had words over a woman and he tried to back-shoot me so I beat him black and blue," Fargo related, watching their faces for their reaction.

"What woman?"

"Reverend Jasmine Honeydew."

"Who?"

It was plain to Fargo that neither had any notion who she was or what was going on. Apparently only Sharpton and those with him had been involved with running her out.

"He stole your horse so you're taking it out on us?" Straw Skimmer asked him.

"I'd shoot any son of a bitch who stole mine," Volcanic said. "We had no part in taking yours."

Fargo suddenly changed his mind. "I believe you. Which is why I want to show you something. When I count to three, draw. I won't shoot you. But you need to know."

"Need to know what?"

"One."

"You pull your pistol on us and I *will* shoot you," Volcanic warned.

"Two."

"This is making no kind of sense," Straw Skimmer said.

"Three."

Both went for their six-shooters. Volcanic was faster than Straw Skimmer and had his hand on the pearl grips of his revolver when the *click* of Fargo's Colt turned both of them to marble.

29

"Jesus!" Straw Skimmer said.

Volcanic's eyes had widened. "Damn. That was the quickest I've ever seen except for maybe Blakely."

Fargo seldom showed off but he did now. He let down the hammer and twirled the Colt forward and backward. He spun it on the tip of his finger and flipped it into the air and caught it by the grips, thumbing back the hammer as he caught it. He spun it so his hand was on top and the pistol was to the floor and then he spun it with his hand under the pistol and the pistol to the ceiling. To finish he did a border shift and smoothly did a reverse twirl into his holster.

"God Almighty," Straw Skimmer breathed.

Volcanic was the smarter of the pair. "You showed us all that so you wouldn't have to kill us."

"I did you a favor," Fargo said. "Now I'd like you to do one for me. Go to your boss and tell him I want my horse back. I'll give him two hours. If it's not back by then, I'll come looking for it and anyone who gets in my way will answer to this." Fargo patted his Colt.

"But it was Sharpton who took it," Straw Skimmer said. "Why threaten Mr. Mitchell?"

"Sharpton works for him, doesn't he?"

Volcanic said, "Mr. Mitchell would never have anyone steal a horse. He's too nice for that."

"Two hours," Fargo repeated. He wheeled and walked toward the batwings, confident neither would try to put a slug in his back. He was glad he hadn't had to shoot them. He hoped his idea worked, and by sending word direct to Mitchell he'd get the Ovaro back without having to hurt anyone. Well, except for Sharpton. Sharpton had to answer for it, no matter what. Pushing on the batwings, he turned left and nearly collided with Reverend Honeydew. "Damn, woman."

"I was worried about you."

"Quit following me." Fargo walked around her and she fell into step next to him.

"Why are you so mad at me?"

"Since I met you I have been threatened and nearly been shot and had a fight and my horse was stolen,"

Fargo recited. "If that's not cause to be mad at someone, I don't know what the hell is."

"None of that was my fault. I'm only here to save the sinners."

Fargo abruptly stopped and faced her. "Let's get something straight. I'm a sinner. I drink. I gamble. I like to be with ladies. I don't suffer fools and I never turn the other cheek. And I don't need to be saved by you or any other do-good."

"You only think you don't."

"Damn it."

"What?"

Fargo walked on. He wished to hell he hadn't helped her back at the stream but he never could stand seeing anyone run roughshod. Women, kids, horses, when he saw them being mistreated, it got his goat. He tried not to let it but so far he couldn't break the habit.

"Permit me to make it up to you by buying you a meal. I haven't had a bite all day and I'm famished."

"No."

"What harm can a meal do?"

The mention of food had made Fargo's stomach rumble. He was hungry, too, and he did have two hours to kill. He stopped and sighed and said, "All right. But I don't want any Bible-pushing."

"You're asking a lot. It is second nature to me. Trying to save souls is what I do."

"We eat and that's all," Fargo said. "You can talk if you want but not about that."

"Very well."

"I mean it, Reverend."

"I would rather you call me Jasmine," she said. "As hard as it will be, I will do as you ask." She smiled sweetly and her whole face glowed. "Consider me putty in your hands."

"Oh hell," Fargo said.

5

Milo served food but he wasn't much of a cook. The steak was rare, the slices of potato had enough grease on them to lubricate a wagon wheel, and the carrots were as close to raw as a cooked carrot could be and still be considered cooked. But the coffee was good and plenty of it, and Fargo needed his head clear after all the whiskey he'd had. He ate in silence and absently listened to Reverend Jasmine Honeydew tell him about her life growing up in New Jersey. *All* about it, from her birth on a cold December morning through her early school years and how she had always liked church more than anything so naturally when she found out that Oberlin College was permitting women to take their theology course, she eagerly enrolled.

"My parents paid for the tuition but I had to support myself otherwise. I don't mind telling you it was a struggle."

Fargo had a struggle of his own going on; a piece of steak with more gristle than meat.

"Do you realize I am only one of twenty women in the entire country to graduate from that course?"

"Good for you."

Jasmine was about to stab a carrot, and looked up. "I am boring you with my past, aren't I?"

"I'm more interested in how you fill out that dress," Fargo bluntly responded.

32

Jasmine's cheeks colored pink. "I ask you to remember I am a woman of the cloth, as they say."

"It's that woman part I like."

"You, sir, are incorrigible." She merrily went on eating and talking. She told him about some of her courses and then mentioned that the woman she most admired in all the world was Joan of Arc.

"Wasn't she a female knight?" Fargo vaguely recollected. He also recalled she had been French.

"She was much more. She was a warrior for God. She had visions in which God told her what to do."

"How much wine did she drink before she had them?"

"Honestly. Joan was devout in her faith. Her visions started when she was twelve. She also heard voices in her head that no one else could hear."

"Ghosts?" Fargo said drily.

"Angels and saints, I think it was. And then God himself spoke to her."

"It must have been crowded in there."

"Where?"

"Between her ears."

Jasmine broke into gay laughter. "You are atrocious. What a horrid thing to say. She was in earnest, I can assure you."

"I met a man once," Fargo said. "An old trapper who said he was exploring Sasty, as they called Mount Shasta back then, and he came on a cave. He followed it for miles to a cavern so big he couldn't see the end of it. There was an underground city with people walking around. They wore long robes and talked in a tongue he didn't savvy and ate strange food. They fed him and sent him on his way. He always wanted to go back but could never find the cave again. He was in earnest, too."

"That's just plain silly."

Fargo looked at her.

"Well, it is. Talking to a bunch of people under the earth isn't the same as talking to angels and the Almighty. And you're missing the whole point. I do what I do because just like Joan of Arc, I have been inspired by God to save the sinful."

"There you go again."

"Why does it bother you so much?"

"Look," Fargo said, and rested his forearms on the edge of the table. "People are free to believe whatever they want. It's how things should be. But they aren't free to shove it down someone else's throat. Especially mine."

"I'm sorry you feel that way. I aim to start a church here in Hapgood Pond. You might not like it. Abe Mitchell might not like it. But I am bound and determined to save these people."

Fargo gazed about the room. Milo was chomping on a cigar and cleaning the bar. Charley was at the corner table, so drunk he had passed out. Maude was back to her solitaire, a bottle of rum at her elbow. "Good luck," he said.

Jasmine forked a piece of carrot so hard it was a wonder she didn't break the plate. "You test me, sir."

"I what?"

"You are a trial. You mock me and belittle my dream and ogle me as if I am a saloon hussy."

"I heard that," Maude said.

"No offense, sister."

"We're not related, dearie. And I don't care what you think of me. I am what I am and I'm happy being me."

"You like spreading your legs for money?"

Maude chuckled. "I would spread them anyway so I might as well be paid for it." She cocked her head. "When was the last time you spread yours?"

"I beg your pardon?"

"You heard me. Parsons and such can have wives. Which means you can take a husband if you're of a mind."

"I'm not," Jasmine flatly declared.

"I didn't think you would be," Maude said. "You're one of those as makes a man get on his knees and beg for it, and you're not content unless he worships you like you do the Almighty."

Jasmine went as stiff as a board. "How dare you?"

"How dare I what? Tell the truth?" Maude laughed.

34

"There are two kinds of women in this world, honey. Those who like it and those who pretend they don't. It's not hard to guess which you are."

"I thought you liked me."

"I do. I respect the hell out of you. But you're still female and females have needs."

"You, madam, are being vulgar."

"I don't even know what that means. But I do know I had a fine time with that handsome slab of muscle across from you, which is more than you'll ever get to say."

"What did I ever do to you that you should talk to me like this?" Jasmine asked.

"I don't like to be looked down on. You sit up there on your high horse and treat the rest of us women as hussies. Your own word, preacher."

Fargo was reminded of a wet hen, the way Jasmine Honeydew was staring at Maude. He speared his last piece of steak and pushed his plate back. "I'm obliged for the meal."

"It was the least I could do."

Fargo noticed that her hands were trembling but whether from anger or something else he couldn't say.

"Would you care to have supper with me tonight, too?"

The invitation surprised him. Fargo didn't think she liked him all that much. "I'm not sure I'll still be around."

"I'll treat you."

"For a minister you are awful free with your money."

"I have a little saved," Jasmine said. "And I like being in your company." She lowered her voice. "That woman was right about one thing. You are easy on the eyes."

"Why, Reverend Honeydew," Fargo said.

Jasmine did more blushing. "I didn't mean that the way you think I meant it."

Before Fargo could ask her what she did mean, hooves drummed in the street. A lot of hooves. Dust swirled past the batwings. Saddles creaked and men shouted. Boots clomped, and shortly someone yelled, "He's not in the general store!" Someone else hollered, "He's not in the Sagebrush!" Then an angular face and a flat-crowned black hat framed the batwings, and in strode Blakely. He took a couple of steps, spotted Fargo, and turned.

"He's in here, Mr. Mitchell."

A shadow fell across the entrance and Fargo expected the man behind his troubles to enter but it was the gunman with the Volcanic revolver who sauntered in, followed by Straw Skimmer and several others. Volcanic nodded at Fargo and said, "I did as you asked."

Next came a man as different from them as night from day. Most of the gun crowd were hard men, bred in violence, and it showed in the way they carried themselves and in the hawklike gleam in their eyes. But the man who came in now was more soft than hard, with a round body in an expensive suit and a bowler. His hair was graying and his cheeks sagged, lending him a hound dog expression. He wore gloves, even though it was summer, and carried a cane.

Volcanic pointed at Fargo. "That's the one, sir. The hombre in the buckskins."

"Thank you, Mr. Quarry," Abe Mitchell said politely. His voice was as soft as his body. He came over, his cane lightly thumping the floorboards with each step.

Fargo was studying him and almost missed Reverend Honeydew's reaction.

She gave a slight start and began to slide her hand under the table but glanced at the other men and stopped.

"I'm Abe Mitchell," the soft man needlessly announced. "Do you mind if I take a seat?"

"Help yourself." Fargo pushed a chair out with his foot.

Mitchell doffed his hat to Jasmine. "I take it you are the minister they told me about?" He turned to Fargo. "And you are the one whose horse was taken by one of my men?"

"Stolen is the word I'd use."

"I don't blame you," Mitchell said with a weary smile. "So I suppose I should attend to you and then deal

36

with the reverend, here." He raised his right hand and snapped his fingers.

Blakely glanced at the batwings. "Get in here," he said.

Fargo nearly came out of his chair. It was Sharpton who entered, his hat in his hands, much of his face black and blue and swollen. He stopped next to Abe Mitchell's chair.

"Tell him," Mitchell said quietly.

Sharpton turned to Fargo and bowed his head. "I'm sorry, mister," he said contritely. "It was wrong of me to take your horse."

Fargo was dumfounded.

"Tell him the rest," Mitchell commanded.

"I only took it so you couldn't leave. I was worried you would ride off and I wouldn't get to repay you for the beating you gave me."

Fargo rose. His fingers twitched, he was so anxious to draw. "I should gun you where you stand."

Abe Mitchell nodded. "You would certainly be within your rights. What he did was deplorable. As soon as he told me I decided to come into Hapgood Pond. We met Mr. Quarry and Mr. Tamblyn on their way out to my place to deliver your message." He paused. "Your horse is outside. A fine animal, that stallion." He motioned. "If you insist on settling accounts with Mr. Sharpton, you are entitled. But I ask you to spare him. No harm has been done except to your pride. That is, if we don't count the condition of Mr. Sharpton's face."

Fargo clenched his fists in anger. This wasn't how he had imagined it turning out.

This wasn't how he imagined it at all.

"If it will help, I can't express how sorry I am. Mr. Sharpton is overzealous at times, I am afraid." Mitchell smiled benignly at Jasmine Honeydew. "He was overzealous with you, Reverend. They are under orders and he carried them too far."

"What orders?" Jasmine asked.

Abe Mitchell sat back and put his hands on his cane.

"In order for you to fully understand, I must explain myself. You see, I have an enemy. A particularly vicious enemy who will stop at nothing to put me under the earth. That is why I have my men keep their eyes out for strangers. Unfortunately, Mr. Sharpton got carried away and decided to run you out before I even knew you were here."

"You have your men run out a lot of people, do you?"

"They do what they must to protect me. I'm afraid that's all I can say on the subject. I ask that you and Mr. Fargo, here, forgive them and forgive me. It should come naturally to you, after all."

"What do you . . ." Jasmine stopped and touched her white collar. "Oh."

"Yes. That," Mitchell said. "Now that I've met you, you have free rein of the settlement and can do as you please."

"I intend to build a church."

"Really?" Abe Mitchell smiled. "All the best, then. Hapgood Pond can use one. The people here are not what you would call God-fearing. Myself excluded, of course."

"Is that so?" Jasmine said skeptically.

"As God is my witness," Mitchell responded. "My parents started taking me to church when I was five. I'm the most religious person I know, except for possibly you."

The more Fargo heard, the less it made sense. "Why is someone out to kill you then?"

"I wish I knew." Mitchell slowly stood. "Both of you can stay in Hapgood Pond for as long as you like. My men won't bother you."

"What about me, boss?" Sharpton asked.

Mitchell turned to Fargo. "Yes. What about him? Will you forgive and forget or must I hire someone to replace him?"

Fargo was about to say he would let it drop when Sharpton said the wrong thing.

"I didn't hurt your horse or anything. I just took him."

"Thanks for reminding me." Fargo slammed his fist

into Sharpton's gut and Sharpton clutched at the table and gurgled and coughed. He half hoped Sharpton would retaliate. He got his wish.

"You shouldn't have done that, you son of a bitch," the gunman snarled, and balled his fists.

Fargo cocked his arm to hit him again.

6

Every now and then Fargo met someone who was so completely different from what he expected, he didn't know what to make of them. Abe Mitchell was an example. Given everything Fargo had heard, he figured Mitchell for one of those who thought they could lord it over others. But Mitchell was the exact opposite; he was soft-spoken, almost timid. As Fargo went to hit Sharpton again, Mitchell put a hand on Sharpton's chest and raised the other in appeal.

"Please. No more. Haven't the two of you beat on one another enough?"

"He deserved that," Fargo said.

"He was in the wrong to take your horse but now your animal is back safe and sound so what is the point in more violence?" Mitchell sadly frowned. "I am so sick of violence, I can't stand the sight of it."

Fargo lowered his arm but his blood was roaring in his veins. "You ask a lot."

"It's the decent thing to do and you strike me as a decent man."

"You're a puzzlement," Fargo said.

Abe Mitchell turned to Sharpton. "From here on out you will not do anything without checking with me first. Or with Mr. Blakely. He is now in charge of those I have hired, not you."

"What? I was only trying to protect you like you wanted," Sharpton protested.

"My decision is final." Mitchell smiled at Reverend Honeydew and nodded at Fargo. "It was nice making your acquaintance." He turned to depart.

"Wait," the minister said. "That's it?"

"What more would you have of me? I've apologized and you are free to stay or go, as you desire."

"I, for one, would like an explanation," she said. "Why did your men try to run me off?"

"I've already explained that," Mitchell said. "I have an enemy."

"Who?"

"That, Reverend, is none of your affair." Mitchell turned on a heel and marched out. Sharpton, crestfallen, followed him.

Blakely, Quarry, and Tamblyn lingered, all three staring at Fargo. Or, in Blakely's case, at Fargo's Colt.

"These two have told me how good you are."

"And?"

"If you're lying to Mr. Mitchell, if you're really here to kill him, you'll answer to me."

"Oh?"

A flick of Blakely's wrist, and the Smith and Wesson was in his hand. He twirled it forward and backward, alternating with lightning speed. He twirled it with his hand under it and with his hand over it. He flipped it, as Fargo had done, and expertly caught it, and spun it into his holster so fast it was a blur.

"God Almighty," Tamblyn said.

Blakely hadn't taken his eyes off Fargo. "That was to let you know what you are up against. One gun hand to another."

"I don't make my living with my gun," Fargo said.

"I do." Blakely smiled at Reverend Honeydew and said, "Ma'am." Then he turned and walked off, his spurs jingling. Tamblyn hastened after him.

Quarry grinned at Fargo and patted his Volcanic. "You two make me feel like a damned amateur. I would try to stop you if you try to hurt Mr. Mitchell, but I wouldn't last two seconds." He scooted after his friends.

"Men," Reverend Honeydew said.

Fargo turned. "What was that?"

"You and your silly ways. What purpose did that exhibition of his have other than to show off?"

"You might say it was a professional courtesy."

"Call it what you will, men are forever trying to beat each other at one thing or another. It's perfectly silly."

"It's good for us you overlook our failings, then," Fargo said.

"I do?"

"Isn't that what ministers are supposed to do?"

"Oh. Yes." Jasmine coughed. "I was only pointing it out. To be honest, I never understood men at all."

Maude was back to her solitaire. "There's not a whole to figure out, dearie. They like to poke and drink and belch. Let them do that and they are pretty much happy."

"There must be more to it than that," Jasmine said.

"Trust me on this, Reverend. Life ain't as complicated as you seem to think. All that education, you should know that."

Fargo walked to the batwings. Abe Mitchell and his men had mounted and reined around to ride out. Mitchell saw him, and smiled. The dust they raised was slow to settle. So were Fargo's thoughts.

Milo had come over and was wiping his hands on a cloth. "Nice man, that Mr. Mitchell."

"Yes," Fargo said. "He is." He regarded the bartender. "What can you tell me about him?"

"Not much. He hired me in Saint Louis. I was tending bar there and he offered me twice as much to come tend bar in the saloon he was opening here. I asked him why he wanted to open one so far away from everywhere when he could make more money running one in a big city and he said a strange thing. He said he liked to have his liquor close."

"He must have money."

"He's well-off, no doubt about that," Milo said. "Gun

42

hands don't come cheap and look at how many he has working for him."

"Why did Mitchell pick *here* of all places?" Fargo wondered out loud.

"He never said. But if you want my opinion, he got tired of looking. We had our own wagon train, close to ten wagons loaded with all his effects and supplies and the goods he needed to start the saloon. We took the Oregon Trail part of the way and then he struck off across the prairie. Here and there he'd come on a spot he liked but none were ever good enough."

"He didn't have it picked in advance?"

"I don't think so, no. I got the impression he was more interested in getting away than going to, if that makes any sense. Anyway, the first time he set eyes on the pond and Charley's cabin and the settlement, which didn't even have a name then, he called us all together and said that we had gone far enough. And here he stayed."

"Those were his exact words? 'Far enough'?"

"Yeah."

"Interesting," Fargo said.

"Isn't it? That was before I heard about this enemy of his."

"Any idea who the enemy is?"

"Not any at all," the bartender said. "Hell, even his gun hands don't know. Which is why they are suspicious of every stranger."

"Did you get to know him well?"

"No. I doubt anyone does. He keeps his secrets to himself. But he sure is nice. His men respect the hell out of him. Half come in every night to drink and play cards and the rest stay at his house and guard him."

"Strange," Fargo said.

"Isn't it, though?" Milo shrugged. "Oh well. He pays good money and it's been peaceful since we got here." He turned. "Stick around. The nights here are right lively."

"I might just do that." Fargo wouldn't mind sleeping in a bed for a change.

He went out and over to the hitch rail in front of the

43

general store; Sharpton had put the Ovaro back where he got him. Fargo patted it and checked his saddlebags and that the Henry was in the saddle scabbard. Everything appeared to be as it should.

The one thing Hapgood Pond didn't have was a stable. Fargo unwrapped the reins and led the stallion over to the pond so it could drink and graze. He sat with his back to a tree, plucked a blade of grass, and stuck the stem between his teeth. He wasn't there two minutes when a man came out of the other saloon, the Sagebrush, caught sight of him, and ambled over with an odd rolling gait, as if he were walking on the deck of a storm-tossed ship. The man was dressed in a store-bought suit. He wore a derby and a bowtie and the chain of a pocket watch hung from a vest pocket.

"How do you do, sir? Malcolm Keever is the name."

Fargo shook without rising. "Let me guess. You're a drummer."

Keever acted surprised. "How did you know?"

"Drummers have a way about them," Fargo said. They dressed like Keever and had a ready smile like Keever and slicked their hair so that it practically dripped, as his did.

"I suppose we do at that," Keever said amiably. "But the same can be said about most any profession, don't you think? Look at bank clerks with their starched shirts and gamblers with their frock coats and doctors with their black bags. They all tend to dress a lot alike." He paused. "Look at yourself. Were I to venture a guess of my own, I would say you are a frontiersman."

Fargo looked down at his buckskins and laughed.

"All right. That wasn't much of a guess," Keever admitted. "Then how about this? Since you're not as smelly as a hide hunter and you don't wear a beaver or coon hat like most trappers do, I'd say you must be a scout."

"Not bad."

"The same can be said of this little hamlet." Keever gestured expansively. "I stumbled on it two days ago and can't bring myself to leave. The days are dull but the nights are a delight."

"Is that so?"

"Don't take my word for it. Stay over and see for yourself. The doves are a cut above the common class and the liquor isn't watered down."

"I aim to stay over tonight," Fargo said.

"You won't regret it. Except for the stabbing, I can't remember any place I've been to, and I've been to most everywhere, where the people are as friendly." Keever reached into a pocket and pulled out a polished silver flask. "I sell these, by the way. The best on the market. They never leak and won't break if they fall out of your pocket. I go from saloon to saloon and convince the owners to put my flasks on display. I don't get rich but I make a comfortable living."

The man was a talker but Fargo was interested in a particular comment. "What was that about a stabbing?"

"The night before last. One of Abe Mitchell's men was found out back of the Blue Heron with a knife in the back of his neck. The strange thing is, he hadn't had a fight with anyone. And he wasn't robbed. Whoever did it just killed him and left him lying there."

"Well, now," Fargo said. No wonder the hired guns were extra protective of Mitchell. Did that mean, he asked himself, that Mitchell's enemy had found him? Or was the knifing a coincidence? "Has anyone else been murdered around here?"

"Not that I know of, no. It has folks a little bit on edge." Keever grinned. "Not me. There's no earthly reason for anyone in this world to want to harm me." He pocketed the flask and turned. "I'll leave you in peace. I just wanted to make your acquaintance."

"And to try and sell me a flask."

"That too." Keever chuckled and strolled toward the saloons.

Fargo took the stem from his mouth and threw it away. He was curious about the killing and curious about Abe Mitchell but whatever was going on in Hapgood Pond had nothing to do with him. He was going to keep his nose out of it and enjoy himself. A bottle or two, a card game or three, and a willing dove would make his night complete. He would sleep and be on his way at first light.

His whole night planned, Fargo leaned back. It had been a while since he could relax. Out in the wilds he always had to be on his guard. At night he slept with his rifle at his side and sometimes with his Colt in his hand.

He pulled his hat low against the glare of the afternoon sun and closed his eyes. It wasn't long before he felt himself dozing off. Just as he was about to, a shuffling sound snapped him awake. Out of habit he dropped his hand to his Colt.

"It's just me," Reverend Honeydew said. "Mind if I join you?"

Fargo did mind but he patted the grass and replied, "I was about to take a nap."

"I'm sorry to intrude." Jasmine primly tucked her legs under her. Smoothing her dress, she smiled sweetly and said, "You're looking at me that way again."

"What way?"

"As if you want to eat me alive."

"You're a good-looking woman. I'm a man."

"That I'm a minister means nothing to you?"

"Nothing at all."

Jasmine frowned. "You are the most brazen man I have ever met. But the truth is, I like you. I like you a great deal."

"Enough to . . . ?" Fargo didn't finish.

"Enough to what?" Jasmine arched her eyebrows. "Oh, Good Lord, no. How can you even think such a thing? I am beginning to understand why most women regard most men as randy goats."

Fargo sighed and folded his arms across his chest. "One of these days you'll grow up."

"I am perfectly mature, thank you very much." Jasmine compressed her lips. "I didn't come out here to argue."

"And you didn't come out here because you're hankering to make love to me."

"Will you please stop? No. I came out because I overheard something I thought you would like to know

46

about since it involved you." Jasmine glanced at the Blue Heron. "That dove and the bartender were talking . . ."

"They have names. Maude and Milo."

"Yes. Those two. He was at her table and they were whispering but I distinctly heard her say that a man had been stabbed here the other night."

"I already heard."

"You did? Do you also know that he was killed with something called an Arkansas toothpick?"

Fargo sat up straight. "What?"

"That's right. I heard Maude tell Milo that you have the exact same kind of knife. She saw it when you two were indulging your carnal lust in her room. And Milo said that they should get word to Abe Mitchell. What do you think of that?"

"Oh hell," Fargo said.

7

Men on the frontier used a lot of different knives: hunting knives, skinning knives, carving knives, folding knives, and endless miscellaneous knives. The most popular was the bowie. Named after the legendary knife fighter who lost his life at the Alamo, the bowie was a formidable weapon in the hands of someone who knew how to use one. A few decades ago bowie schools had sprung up all over the country, where the art of cut and gut was taught to thousands. There weren't as many of those schools now but the bowie was still held in high regard.

The Arkansas toothpick saw a lot of use, too, principally in the South where in some states it rivaled the bowie for popularity. West of the Mississippi there weren't as many to be found but enough that it was fairly common.

The two knives were considerably different in design. Bowies were big, some with blades fifteen inches or longer. They had a single cutting edge although some had a short edge on the top near the tip. Toothpicks were always doubled-edged from hilt to point. And toothpicks came in all lengths. There were some as big as bowies. There were middling-sized toothpicks. And there were small, slim toothpicks, like the one Fargo wore in his ankle sheath.

A lot of men relied on them. So it wasn't unusual that one of Abe Mitchell's gun hands had been killed with a toothpick. What was unusual, though, was that the knife had been left in the man's neck. That was careless. Knives cost money.

It suggested the killer had been drunk and forgotten it.

Or so Skye Fargo thought as he sat pondering. Pushing to his feet, he went to the Ovaro and took hold of the reins.

"Going somewhere?" Reverend Honeydew asked.

Fargo didn't answer. He frowned when she came with him. "Don't you have preaching to do?"

"My, my. I come out to warn you and you treat me as if I have the plague. Is that any way to repay me?"

Again Fargo didn't answer.

"Was Maude telling the truth? Do you have an Arkansas toothpick?"

"Yes," Fargo begrudgingly confirmed.

"Can I see it?"

"What the hell for?"

"I'd just like to know what one looks like. I don't pay much attention to knives."

"No."

"Why not?"

"I don't need a reason."

"Goodness, you are touchy," Jasmine said. "I don't see why you are so upset. It wasn't your knife that killed that poor man."

"Abe Mitchell might think different."

"Ah. You're worried he'll come back in with all his men to have another talk with you? Or maybe string you up, vigilante style?"

"Mitchell doesn't strike me as the stringing kind," Fargo said.

"If there is anything I can do to help you, just say so. I'll remind Mr. Mitchell that you weren't here two nights ago. That should suffice to clear you of suspicion."

"You've never seen a lynch mob." Not that Fargo expected it to come to that. If Mitchell really believed he was to blame, Mitchell would send his top gun hand, the best in his employ. Mitchell would send Blakely.

Jasmine breathed deep and gazed at the blue sky and said, "It's a glorious day, isn't it? Days like this always make me thankful for being alive."

If Fargo didn't know any better, he would almost think she was poking fun at him. He came to the hitch rail in front of the Blue Heron and tied off the Ovaro. A few more customers had trickled in, and every last one glanced at him.

Word was spreading. He made straight for Maude's table. She was still playing solitaire. Without being asked he pulled out a chair and sat across from her. "I didn't kill Mitchell's man."

Maude went on playing. "I never said you did. All I said was that I noticed you wear the same kind of knife that killed him. I should know. I found the body."

"You know how people are. Everyone will think I was to blame."

"No one will do anything. Not without proof."

"Damn it, Maude."

She looked up, a black queen in her hand. "Listen. I like you. I believe you when you say you didn't do it. But you could have. You could have snuck in and killed Tyler and snuck off again and showed up here today with that snooty preacher."

"He was a gun hand?"

"Tyler? No. From what I hear, Tyler worked for Mitchell before Mitchell came west. They were good friends. Mitchell took it hard."

"And you had to go and tell Milo." Fargo got up and went over to the bar. Milo was pouring for another customer and took his time placing the bottle of brandy back on the shelf and coming over.

"What can I get for you?"

"Have you already sent word to Mitchell about my toothpick?"

Milo put on a poker face. "I don't know what you're talking about."

"You don't want to make me mad."

"I still don't know what you're talking about."

Fargo drew his Colt and set it on the bar with a thud, his fingers splayed over the grips. "I need to know."

"You won't shoot me. Not in front of witnesses you won't."

"Ever seen someone pistol-whipped?"

Milo glanced at the Colt and blanched. "I work for Abe. And I like him. He's a good man. A decent man."

"So you did send word already," Fargo said, and swore.

"Not that I think you had anything to do with killing Tyler," Milo quickly said. "But I had to let Mr. Mitchell know. You can see that, can't you?"

Fargo holstered the Colt and strode out. He blinked in the harsh glare of the sun and stepped to the hitch rail and drew up short. Reverend Honeydew was on her horse, which was next to the Ovaro, her reins in hand. "What do you think you're doing?"

"Riding out to Abe Mitchell's with you. I figured you would want to go talk to him and set things straight."

"You did, did you?" Fargo said, his tone making it plain he had no intention of taking her along.

"It's in your best interest to take me. He's less apt to have his men gun you if I'm along." She bestowed a beatific smile. "Surely you have heard that blessed are the peacemakers? I can make peace between the two of you."

Fargo was about to tell her to go ride her horse into the pond, but on second thought, he changed his mind. It could be she was right. Her presence might dampen any desire on Mitchell's part or the part of Mitchell's men to shoot him on sight.

"What do you say? May I or may I not?"

"Just so you don't talk me to death." Fargo stepped into the stirrups and reined away from the rail. He rode on past the last of the buildings and struck off to the east along a rutted track scoured bare by hooves.

Jasmine came up next to him. She sat a horse uncommonly well, her curly hair cascading over her shoulders, her dress clinging to the contours of her thighs. "You're welcome," she said.

"Did I miss something?" Fargo couldn't take his eyes off her thighs. For a minister she was downright gorgeous.

"You didn't thank me for helping you. I assume it's because you have so much else on your mind but I knew that you would if you had thought of it."

"You take an awful lot for granted."

Jasmine laughed.

Fargo liked this side of her. She was always the stern parson hell-bent on wiping out sin. It was nice to see she could be a woman, as well. He admired the sweep of her bosom and how her leg molded to the saddle.

"You're doing it again."

"I'm male."

"So you keep reminding me." She regarded him a moment. "But is that *all* you ever think of?"

"I think about whiskey and cards."

"I can see that trying to change you is hopeless. I have about as much chance of making a churchgoer out of you as I do of turning water into wine."

"You never know," Fargo said. "If all the ladies at church were as good-looking as you . . ."

Jasmine really had a nice laugh. "That would defeat the whole purpose. People go to church to be inspired in their faith, not to undress the opposite sex with their eyes."

"You might be surprised."

They came over a rise and their good spirits evaporated. Fargo rose in the stirrups and counted six riders galloping toward them. Three he recognized: Sharpton, the pain in the ass; Quarry, the gunman who favored a pearl-handled Volcanic revolver; and Tamblyn, the man who wore the straw skimmer. He drew rein to await them and Reverend Honeydew did the same. As he came to a stop he placed his right hand on his hip above his Colt.

"Trouble, you think?" Jasmine said.

One of the riders, Fargo saw, wore a suit and a bowler

and no gun belt. The messenger Milo had sent, he suspected. "We'll soon find out."

"Don't worry. I won't let them harm you."

"Plan to shoot them, do you?"

"Heavens, no. I am a woman of the cloth. I will shield you with the word of the Lord."

"I'll put my trust in my Colt."

"Oh ye of little faith."

The rumble of hooves nearly drowned her out. The riders swept toward them and drew rein in a swirl of dust. Fargo stared at the townsman in the bowler and the man tried to shrink into his suit. "Gents," he said.

Sharpton's right hand was close to his Beaumont-Adams revolver. "You're coming with us."

"Is that a fact?"

Sharpton nodded. "Mr. Mitchell wants a word with you and sent us to fetch you whether you want to come or not."

"I'm on my way to see him."

"I'll bet you are." Sharpton let his reins drape over the saddle and held out his left hand. "We'll take that six-shooter of yours."

"No," Fargo said. "You won't."

"We're not asking, mister. We are five guns to your one." Sharpton waggled his hand. "Hand it over."

"I am mighty tired of you."

Sharpton eyes glittered with spite. "Mr. Mitchell made me eat crow earlier and I hated it. Now he sent me to bring you in and that's exactly what I aim to do, my way."

Quarry broke in with, "Mr. Mitchell never said anything about taking his six-gun."

"He left the doing of it up to me," Sharpton said. "And I want this bastard's damn pistol."

"Forget it," Quarry advised. "You haven't seen him draw. I have. The only one of us who can match him is Blakely and he's back at the house."

"You scare too easy."

Jasmine cleared her throat. "Please be reasonable, Mr. Sharpton."

"Stay out of this, lady."

"I will not. And I expect some respect. You will call me Reverend Honeydew, if you please."

Sharpton looked mad enough to chew nails. "I'll call you any damn thing I want. I don't believe in your hokum. To me you're no better than those swindlers who go around selling medicine made of snake oil and swamp water."

"Don't talk to her like that," Quarry said.

Sharpton only got madder. "Who do you work for, anyway? Mr. Mitchell or this bitch?"

Reverend Honeydew suddenly gigged her horse up next to Sharpton's and slapped him across the face. Not lightly, either. She slapped him so hard, her hand left an imprint on his cheek.

Sharpton was as amazed as the rest of them. He put a hand to his face and blurted, "You hit me!"

Reverend Honeydew appeared at a loss for words. She looked at her hand and then at him and said contritely, "I'm sorry, truly sorry."

"I have half a mind to beat you," Sharpton said, and balled his fist.

Fargo was set to intervene but Quarry brought his mount around so that he was facing Sharpton, his hand on the Volcanic. "You so much as touch her and you answer to me."

"What the hell has gotten into you?" Sharpton fumed.

"Where I come from we don't mistreat womenfolk."

"Son of a bitch," Sharpton said.

"Please stop your swearing," Reverend Honeydew requested. "I find it most offensive."

Sharpton glowered at her and said, "Son of a bitch, son of a bitch, son of a bitch."

"You are not a nice man," Reverend Honeydew said.

"Jesus." Sharpton gestured savagely at Quarry. "Shut her up. You hear me? Shut her up or by God I will."

"Reverend," Quarry said.

"I have a perfect right to say whatever I want."

"Enough!" Sharpton exploded. He swung toward Fargo. "This is the last time I will tell you. Hand over your six-shooter. Now."

"No," Fargo said.

"To hell with you, then," Sharpton snarled, and flashed his right hand to the Beaumont-Adams.

8

Fargo expected him to try. Sharpton was one of those people who never learned. Even when it was as plain as the nose on their face that they were making the biggest mistake of their life, they still went ahead and made it. He had the Colt out before Sharpton cleared leather and shot him square in the center of his forehead. Sharpton's hat and a goodly portion of his hair and brains exploded out the back of his head and the body keeled from the horse and flopped to the ground.

The others froze. Fargo slowly moved the Colt's muzzle from right to left and back again. "Anyone else?"

"He had that coming," Quarry said.

Tamblyn spat. "None of us liked him much. But now I suppose we'll have to tote him back and bury him."

Reverend Honeydew had a peculiar expression. She seemed to be fascinated by the exit wound, by the gore and the blood and the brains. "The wicked bring justice down on themselves," she said.

Fargo replaced the spent cartridge and shoved the Colt into his holster. He waited while two of the men threw the body over the saddle and tied the arms and legs so it wouldn't slide off.

"You are awfully quick," Jasmine said to him.

"Practice," Fargo said.

"No. It is more than that. You must possess exceptional reflexes to draw and shoot as fast as you do."

"You're quick, yourself, with that hand of yours." Fargo was only half joking.

"I know I shouldn't have. It goes against everything I believe. But I'm only human, and he got me mad, insulting me as he did."

"That's nice to know," Fargo said.

"What is?"

"That you're human." He grinned and winked.

"You are unbelievable."

Quarry grabbed the reins to Sharpton's mount. He reined alongside the Ovaro and said, "Ready when you are. But one thing before we go." He nodded at Fargo's Colt. "I've seen you draw twice now."

"And?"

"You're faster than any of us except maybe Blakely. So if Mr. Mitchell decides you need killing, I'll have to do you as I'd do Blakely."

"How do you mean?"

"I'll shoot you in the back."

Jasmine was indignant. "What a terrible thing to say. Only a coward would do something like that."

"No, ma'am, it's common sense," Quarry said politely. "I don't stand a chance against him in a straight-up fight. So I'll do the job any way I can."

"But in the back," Jasmine said.

"I'd make it painless," Quarry said. "I'd shoot him in the head."

"How noble of you."

"I didn't reckon you would understand, you being a minister, and all. But a man does what he has to."

Fargo gigged the Ovaro. He didn't like having the gunmen at his back but they were under orders to take him to see their boss so he doubted he would get that slug in the back before then. The reverend stayed on his right and Quarry on his left. The latter kept glancing at him and finally he said, "Admiring my beard?"

The gunman chuckled. "I'm trying to make up my mind about you. You don't strike me as the kind to stab a man from behind."

"You'd shoot me from behind," Fargo said.

"That's different. I'd need to. But as quick as you are, you can take just about anybody face-to-face. Especially Tyler, the man who was knifed. He was from back east and he was no shucks with a six-shooter at all. Half the time he didn't even wear one."

"Yet someone stabbed him anyway?"

"Surprised the hell out of me," Quarry said. "Tyler was almost as nice as Mr. Mitchell, and you've seen how he is."

"What I don't savvy," Fargo said, "is why anyone would want to make maggot bait of a man like him."

"Makes two of us," Quarry said. "It's about driving Blakely loco. He takes his job serious, and his job is keeping Mr. Mitchell alive."

"Will he shoot me in the back too?"

"Blakely? Hell, no. He'll come right up to you and tell you to draw and then it will be over."

"One way or the other," Fargo said.

"I've seen him draw a lot of times when he's practicing. He's a shade quicker than you. Not much, but he doesn't have to be, does he?"

No, Fargo mentally agreed, he didn't. All it took was a split-second's edge. "You'd put your money on him?"

"Every last cent."

Abe Mitchell's house was like the man himself; it wasn't at all as Fargo expected. He'd reckoned on a large house with a stable and maybe a blacksmith shop and a bunkhouse for the riders and outbuildings. But the house was modest. There was a stable and a bunkhouse for Mitchell's protectors but both were as modest as the house. If Mitchell was wealthy, he didn't spoil himself.

Gunmen were lounging in front and about the yard. They converged around the horse bearing the body, and the glances they shot at Fargo didn't bode well. One of them stepped in front of the Ovaro, and glared. He had a salt-and-pepper chin and a crooked nose and a revolver tucked under his belt next to the buckle instead of in a holster.

"Sharpton was my pard, mister. Was it you who gunned him?"

Before Fargo could answer, Quarry spoke up, "Back off, Weaver. Mr. Mitchell wants to talk to him."

"It was him, wasn't it?" Weaver demanded.

Fargo said, "It was me."

Weaver nodded. "We have a score to settle. It won't be now. But you'll pay for Sharpton. You'll pay like you've never paid for anything."

"Quit your blustering," Quarry said.

Weaver jabbed a finger at him. "You're not the boss, boy. You don't tell me what to do." Angrily hitching at his belt, he stalked off.

"Better watch him," Quarry warned. "He's a mean cuss."

"Just what I needed," Fargo said.

The front door opened. Out came Abe Mitchell. Behind him was Blakely. They crossed the porch to the steps and Mitchell saw the body and a look of great sadness came over him.

"Not another one."

"Your doing?" Blakely said to Fargo.

Quarry spoke up for him. "Sharpton was to blame. He prodded and pushed and tried to shoot him."

Abe Mitchell ran a hand over his face. "I made it clear I wanted Mr. Fargo unharmed."

"Sharpton didn't give a damn, boss," Quarry said.

Mitchell closed his eyes and gave a slight tremble. Opening them again, he said, "I can't tell you how sorry I am. Won't you come in? And you too, Reverend. Mr. Quarry, will you see to the grave?"

Fargo turned to Quarry. "Thanks for sticking up for me."

The young gunman shrugged. "I'll still shoot you in the back if I have to. But I hope I don't."

Fargo dismounted and noticed that Reverend Honeydew was still on her horse and staring at him expectantly. "What?"

"A gentleman would help a lady down."

Fargo sighed and held up his arms and she slid into them. The warmth of her body and the brush of her bosom on his chest prompted tantalizing images.

"Thank you." She smoothed her dress and fluffed her hair. "And you can quit that. I'm not an apple pie."

There was a rug in the parlor, and a settee and a grandfather clock, common furnishings, not at all the kind a rich man would have. Fargo sat on the settee with Reverend Honeydew. Mitchell sat in a chair, his hands in his lap. Blakely stood over by the door, his thumbs hooked in his gun belt, a wolf guarding a lamb.

"Now, then," their host began, "permit me to apologize, once again, for Mr. Sharpton. As you know, he was always a bit of a hothead."

"More than a bit," Fargo said.

"I should have sent Mr. Blakely, I suppose, but he insists on not straying far from my side now that I've put him in charge."

"You have more gun sharks than a hound has fleas," Fargo said.

"With good cause, sir, I assure you."

"What cause?" Fargo asked.

Mitchell crossed his legs and placed a hand on his knee. "Before we go any further, might I be permitted to see the Arkansas toothpick I have been told you carry?"

Fargo hesitated. He liked to keep the toothpick a secret. It had saved his life on more occasions than he could count only because no one knew he had it. That it was now common knowledge was bothersome.

"I'll give it right back," Mitchell promised.

Fargo hiked his pant leg, palmed the knife, and reversed his grip so he was holding it by the blade.

Abe Mitchell took it and hefted it and studied the blade and handle. "You take good care of it. There's no rust and it's amazingly sharp." He held it out to Blakely. "What do you think? It looks different than the others to me but I'd like your opinion."

The top gun came over and examined the toothpick closely. "The hilt is walnut. The toothpick that killed Tyler had a rosewood hilt." He gave the toothpick back to his employer and returned to his station by the doorway.

"There you have it," Mitchell said, and extended the

toothpick to Fargo. "I have imposed on you for nothing." He paused. "But where are my manners?" He clapped his hands and a woman in an apron appeared. "Rosie, tea for the lady and coffee for my other guest."

"I'd rather have coffee, too," Reverend Honeydew said.

"As you wish." Mitchell motioned and Rosie departed. He sat back in his chair and rubbed a hand across his face as he had done out on the porch.

"You look worn to a frazzle," Fargo remarked.

"If you only knew." Mitchell smiled a thin smile. "And I suppose you should, now that I have imposed on you. It's an incredible tale. So incredible, I can hardly believe it, myself, and I'm the one whose life is forfeit if my enemy ever finds me."

"Who the hell is this enemy of yours?"

"If I only knew." Mitchell settled back. "I'm from New Orleans, Mr. Fargo. Have you ever been there?"

"Yes."

"A fine city, wouldn't you agree? A bustling port and business center. One hundred and seventy thousand people live there. I was one of them. I was in the textile trade. I had a family I adored and they adored me. I was fairly prosperous and immensely happy."

"You were blessed," Reverend Honeydew said.

"I thought I was, yes," Abe Mitchell said. "Then about three years ago it started. That's when . . ." He stopped. Tears filled his eyes. He looked away as if embarrassed. "Sorry. But when I think of them, it's all I can do not to break down."

"Think of who?" she prompted.

"My wife and my son. You see, they were murdered." Mitchell closed his eyes and put a thumb and a finger on his eyelids. "God. I don't know how much longer I can endure this."

Reverend Honeydew got up and put her hand on his shoulder. "Is there anything I can do?"

"Thank you, no." Mitchell coughed and lowered his hand and gave each of them a weak smile. "I'm sorry. I'm behaving poorly."

"If you would rather not talk about it . . ."

"No. It's all right. Mr. Fargo has a right to know." Mitchell took a deep breath. "I came home from work one day and found my wife dead in our kitchen. She had a knife stuck in the back of her neck."

"My word! Who would do such a thing?"

"I don't know, Reverend," Mitchell said. "I got along well with everyone. The police tried their best to find the murderer but there were no clues to go on. We weren't robbed. Nothing was taken from the house. They decided it must be the work of a lunatic."

"You poor man."

"I should have sold the house and moved to another part of the city. But there were so many memories of Louise—that was my wife's name—that I couldn't bear to sell. I hired a nanny to watch over my son, who was twelve, and picked up the pieces of my life. Months went by. Then on a cold winter's night I came home and the nightmare repeated itself, only worse."

"How could it be worse?" Reverend Honeydew said.

"I found my son and the nanny, dead. Both with knives in the backs of their necks. Exactly like my sweet Louise."

Fargo had been content to listen but now he leaned forward and asked, "What *kind* of knives?"

"Arkansas toothpicks with rosewood hilts."

"All of them?"

Mitchell nodded. "They have all been identical." He rose and stepped to a desk in the corner. Opening the top drawer, he reached in and returned with an Arkansas toothpick in his palm, just as he had described. "This is the one that killed my good friend Eric Tyler."

Reverend Honeydew was horrified. "Four people, foully murdered. What is this world coming to?"

"Would that it were so few," Abe Mitchell said.

"How many has it been?"

Fargo had seen more than his share of killing, and done more than his share, but even he was surprised by Mitchell's answer.

"Eleven."

9

The next to die after Abe Mitchell's son and nanny was his older brother. A worker found him slumped over his desk in his office, an Arkansas toothpick stuck in the back of his neck. After him it was Abe's younger brother and then his sister.

All murdered the same way.

"I was practically beside myself," Abe told them. "The authorities had no idea who was to blame. Neither did I."

"You had to have made an enemy somewhere," Fargo said. It was the only explanation.

"If I did, I didn't know it." Mitchell wrung his hands in despair. "In my business dealings I was always honest and fair."

"What about your personal life?" Reverend Honeydew asked. "Did you ever dally with other women?"

Mitchell reacted as if she had punched him. "How can you even ask such a thing? I loved my wife dearly. I would never be with another woman behind her back. It just wasn't in me." He went on to relate how the manager of the textile company he ran was the next victim, discovered slumped over a yarn-sizer with a toothpick jutting from the base of his skull.

"That makes seven," Reverend Honeydew said.

"Eight and nine were men in my employ," Mitchell went on. "By then it was obvious someone was out to destroy me."

"Tyler was the eleventh?"

Mitchell nodded.

"Who was the tenth?"

"My mother."

"No!"

Abe Mitchell bowed his head and the tears flowed. He cried shamelessly, sniffling now and again. When he could, he cleared his throat and said softly, "She was the straw that broke me. My father had passed on a decade earlier and she lived by herself. She loved flowers and birds and taking a stroll in a park near her house." He choked off, then resumed. "That's where they found her, in the park, sprawled over a bench with another of those damnable knives in the back of her neck. The sweetest, kindest woman you would ever want to meet . . ." He couldn't go on.

Reverend Honeydew squeezed his shoulder and opened her mouth to say something but apparently words failed her and she frowned and touched her white collar.

Fargo had learned a lot but there was a lot more he wanted to learn. He waited for Mitchell to stop weeping before he asked, "How does all that tie in with you being out here in the middle of nowhere?"

"Put yourself in my shoes. I had lost everyone near and dear to me. My business was suffering. After my manager and those two workers were killed, most of my other workers walked out. I can't blame them." Mitchell stood and went to the window and gazed out across the prairie, his hands behind his back. "I didn't want anyone else to die on my account. So I sold my house and my business and came west with Eric Tyler. I thought I was safe here."

"How did the killer find you?" Reverend Honeydew asked.

Fargo was wondering the same thing. They were over a thousand miles from New Orleans.

"I have no idea. Tyler was the only one aware of my plight. The gunmen we hired along the way only knew that someone was after me. I never gave them the particulars."

"So you built this house intending to spend the rest of your days here?" Fargo said.

"I still intend to spend them here. I have too much invested. Too much money, that is. I've used nearly all I had. I have enough to pay Mr. Blakely and his associates for several more months. After that . . ." Mitchell shrugged.

"This isn't New Orleans," Fargo said. "It should be easier to figure out who knifed your friend."

"Some of my men think you were to blame," Abe Mitchell said.

"He wasn't even here then," Reverend Honeydew said.

Mitchell turned. "Do you have proof he wasn't?"

"Well, no. I only just met him on the trail this morning. I can't say where he was before that."

Mitchell said to Fargo. "Truth is, I don't think you are the murderer. You have the look of the wild places about you. I very much doubt you've spent the last three years in New Orleans."

"It must be someone in Hapgood Pond," the reverend suggested.

"That was my first thought," Mitchell said. "Twenty-seven people now call it home. Plus the farmers and the like. Those who were here before I came, I can eliminate."

"Don't forget your gun hands," Fargo said.

"Eh?" Mitchell was taken aback. "I hadn't thought of that but you're right. It could very well be one of the men I hired to protect me. Some of them I hired in New Orleans." He chewed on his lower lip, then said, "And now I'd very much like to hire you."

"I'm a scout, not a gun hand," Fargo set him straight. "I track. I guide. I find people."

"Exactly the skills that might prove useful if the monster who is terrorizing me kills again."

"I don't know," Fargo said. He still didn't want to get involved.

"I will pay you a thousand dollars."

"That's a lot of money."

"And worth it if you can end my nightmare. When the killer strikes again, you will hunt him down."

"When and not if?" Reverend Honeydew said.

"After all this time and all the murders, is there any doubt there will be another?"

Fargo could use the thousand but he had someplace to be and it was a long ride. "You're clutching at straws."

"I freely admit that I am, yes," Mitchell said. "You are my last hope. I could run but I'm tired of running. I will make my stand here, come what may." He came over to the settee. "What do you say?"

"I need to think about it," Fargo hedged.

"Very well. Give me your answer in the morning." Mitchell held out his hand. "Whatever you decide, I thank you for hearing me out." He shook warmly.

"Now if you will excuse me, I'll go say a few words over Mr. Sharpton. He was a hothead but he was working for me and I owe him that much." He turned to Honeydew. "Unless you would rather do it. A eulogy is more in your line of work, I would imagine."

"I'll be glad to. Let me get my Bible out of my saddlebags."

Fargo followed them out. Blakely came last. They stopped on the porch as Mitchell and the minister moved toward a low knoll where several men were wielding shovels.

"For what it's worth," Blakely said, "I don't think you had a hand in it, either."

"Any idea who it could be?"

"If I did they'd be dead. Eric Tyler was a good man. Abe Mitchell is a saint."

"No one walks on water."

"Mitchell comes as close as anyone I've met. You've seen how he is. He's nice to everyone no matter how they treat him. You don't come across many men like him."

"You're taking this personal," Fargo observed.

Blakely frowned. "I reckon I am." He started to go after his employer but stopped. "Are you going to take him up on his offer?"

"He has you," Fargo said. "He doesn't need me."

"I'm no tracker. You have a talent I don't. Nose around. See what you can find. I'll tell the rest that you are not to be bothered and whoever gives you trouble answers to me."

"I don't know."

"What can it hurt?" Blakely went down the steps. "Tyler was killed in the settlement. He'd left here about two hours before. One of the men saw him ride off and thought he heard another rider off a ways."

"He didn't go look?"

"It was dark. He figured it was one of us. We come and go all the time."

Blakely glanced toward the knoll. "I have to go watch over Mitchell."

Fargo leaned on the rail. He decided he would look around a little, just to see what he could find. He forked leather, reined around the house to the rear, and set out in a wide loop, scouring the prairie for sign. It occurred to him that if there had been an unknown rider that night, whoever it was had been spying on the house and saw when Eric Tyler left. He drew rein and surveyed the terrain. The house was now west of him, the knoll where the funeral was being held to the southwest. To the east the ground was essentially flat with islands of trees speckling the sea of grass. To the north, in the distance, were hills. To the south the land was broken by gullies. Here and there were patches of mesquite.

Fargo rode to the south. He came to a gully that offered an unobstructed view of the house and the bunkhouse, a perfect place for someone to lurk. He rode down into it and along the winding bottom, bent low over the saddle. Almost immediately he spied the tracks of a shod horse. "Well, look at this," he said out loud. Dismounting, he knelt and examined them, then walked on leading the Ovaro by the reins. At one spot the grass had been trampled and cropped, suggesting the horse had been tied for a spell. He let the reins drop and climbed to the top. Near the edge was bare dirt. Scrapes showed where someone had been lying.

Fargo was about to go back down when he spied something in the grass. He bent and picked it up. Whoever had been there had smoked a long, thin, cheap cigar. He sniffed it and threw it back down. It was helpful to know but didn't mean much. A lot of men smoked the same kind. He went down and climbed back on the Ovaro. The tracks led to a bend where the rider had gone up and out. Fargo did the same. Predictably, the hoofprints led him to the rutted track that led into Hapgood Pond.

Fargo swung wide in another loop. There might be more sign. He came on a different gully that twisted and turned like a snake. The bottom wasn't marked by tracks so he moved on. Around him the prairie teemed with life. Butterflies flitted on the breeze. A pair of swallows dived for insects. Somewhere a killdeer cried. Prairie dogs whistled and darted into their burrows. He breathed deep of the smell of life.

Fargo loved the wild. More than cards, more than drink, even more than women. He grinned at the notion. Maybe not more than women. He could give up cards and drink if he had to, but the ladies? As honey was to a bear, as nectar to a bee, women were to him. He gazed toward the now far-off knoll where Reverend Honeydew was silhouetted against the sky. And a fine silhouette it was. She had the kind of body men drooled over. A shame, he mused, that she was more passionate about the Almighty than she was about men.

Fargo shook his head. He was letting himself be distracted. Focusing, he saw old buffalo tracks and came on an old wallow. It didn't reek of urine, as a fresh wallow would. He skirted it and roved to the west. The glare of the sun prompted him to pull his hat brim lower. As he did, he glanced to the northwest and happened to catch a bright glimmer. The kind caused by sunlight reflecting off metal.

Fargo reined toward it. There wasn't much cover but that couldn't he helped. He had to cross nearly a quarter mile of open ground. Whoever it was would see him and likely skedaddle.

The glimmer had come from a stand of cottonwoods.

Fargo palmed his Colt as he approached. A robin took wing and then some sparrows. Slowing, he thumbed back the hammer. The stand was roughly oval, and thick with brush. He went around the edge. A break betrayed where someone had gone in. Shod tracks confirmed it. He drew rein and raised the Colt.

The stand was quiet. Alighting, Fargo cautiously entered the break.

A bee buzzed his ear. A garter snake slithered off. Crushed brush pinpointed where a man and a horse had been. He examined the tracks. Some tracks were older than others. Whoever it was had been to the stand more than once. It was another convenient spot from which to spy on the house.

Fargo hurried to the Ovaro, holstered the Colt, and climbed on. The lurker couldn't have gotten far. He reined toward the settlement and within twenty yards came on a dry wash. It explained how the man slipped away unseen. He trotted along the rim, alert for more gleams of light. The killer favored a toothpick but might just as well resort to a rifle.

The wash ended. The rider had come up out of it and made for low hills to the northwest.

Fargo brought the Ovaro to a gallop. He was confident he could overtake his quarry. Few horses equaled the stallion's speed and stamina.

Once past the first hill the tracks pointed to the west, toward Hapgood Pond. Their spacing and clods of dirt told Fargo the lurker was pushing his mount at a gallop.

Fargo used his spurs. The killer was just ahead. He was sure of it. Any moment he would see him. He could almost feel the thousand dollars in his poke. He grinned. He hadn't expected it to be this easy.

In the distance a rider appeared, raising dust.

"I've got you, you son of a bitch," Fargo crowed. He thought of Abe Mitchell's account, and of how many had been murdered, and he reminded himself not to get cocky.

The rider went around a far hill.

The Ovaro flew. Fargo came to the hill and swept

around it. On the far side part of the slope had broken away. Heavy rain, probably, was the cause. Fargo had to swing around an earthen bank as high as his head. As he swept around the end of it, a figure heaved up and launched itself at him.

Surprise delayed his stab for his Colt. Because the figure wasn't a white man.

It was a Sioux warrior.

10

The warrior's shoulder slammed into Fargo, knocking him from the saddle.

A tomahawk flashed at his head. Fargo caught the warrior's wrist as he fell, stopping the edge an inch from his face. He tried to turn in midair so that he was on top and the warrior was on the bottom but he succeeded only in twisting them partway; they landed on their sides. The warrior sought to wrest his arm loose and drove a knee at Fargo's gut. Fargo couldn't avoid it. His stomach exploded in pain.

It bought the warrior the split second he needed to scramble onto his other knee. Fargo punched him on the jaw. The warrior struggled to free his wrist, and Fargo, lunging, seized hold of the warrior's long hair and levered himself off the ground. With a hiss of fury, the warrior clawed his fingers at Fargo's eyes. Fargo jerked his face away and the tip of one of the fingers poked into his mouth. He clamped down with his teeth and felt the crunch of bone and tasted the spurt of blood. The warrior yelped and pulled his hand back.

Fargo spit out the fingertip. He hit the warrior again, on the cheek, and a third time, on the temple. The Sioux were superb fighters but they didn't use their fists much. The warrior made no attempt to block the punches. Fargo boxed him above the ear and the warrior sagged. His fist was hurting like hell but Fargo struck again, unleashing an uppercut. Suddenly the warrior was on his back, barely conscious. Fargo wrenched the tomahawk from his grasp, took a step back, and drew his Colt.

The Sioux was a while recovering. His hair, his buckskins, his moccasins identified him as a Minniconjou.

Fargo scoured the prairie but saw no sign of any others. The Ovaro had stopped a dozen yards away and was looking back. He whistled and it came to him. Snatching the reins, he climbed on and again looked around but still saw no one. He kept the Colt trained on the Minniconjou.

Presently the man grunted and blinked his eyes. He slowly sat up, rubbed his jaw, and tilted his head up at Fargo. "Kill me, white man," he said defiantly. "It is a good day to die."

"It would be a shame to kill so brave a warrior."

The Minniconjou was startled. "You speak our tongue?"

"I speak it well. I lived with the Lakotas once. It was a happy time in my life."

The warrior grew thoughtful. "I have heard of a white man who lived with Those-Who-Plant-By-The-Water. Was that you?"

"Unless there was another white, yes."

"I am glad I did not kill you, then. They say that you have a good heart. That you are a friend to all Lakotas."

"If they are friends to me," Fargo said. "But you came at me as an enemy. You tried to count coup on me."

"I am Eats-With-Bear," the warrior introduced himself. "I did not know who you were. I have followed you for many sleeps thinking only that you are a white man and I must slay you."

"You were with the war party that chased me," Fargo guessed.

"*Han*," Eats-With-Bear replied, which was Lakota for "yes."

"The others gave up but you did not."

"*Heyah*." Lakota for "no."

"Why?"

"They knew you would reach the white village before they could catch you. And their horses were tired."

"I meant why did you keep after me?"

"I wanted your horse. It is the finest I have ever seen. It has much *tinza*. It goes far and never tires. I would have made it my warhorse and done many brave deeds in battle. My people would sing praises of me." Eats-With-Bear nodded at the stallion. "And it is a *shunke-kan*. As you must know, my people like them."

"*Heyah*," Fargo said.

"No?"

"It is not a pinto."

"It looks like a pinto," Eats-With-Bear insisted.

"The markings are different," Fargo explained. He patted the stallion's neck. "My horse is an Ovaro."

"O-var-o? That is a white word?"

"It is Spanish."

"I thought so."

Fargo got back to the matter that interested him most. "You followed me to the white village and watched for me until you saw me leave?"

"Yes. With the white woman. Is she yours?"

"She is a friend." Fargo almost added in English, "of sorts."

"She is ugly," Eats-With-Bear declared. "She is too tall and too pale and her hair could use bear fat."

"True," Fargo said.

Eats-With-Bear rose to his feet. "You are my enemy no longer. From this day on we will be friends."

Fargo believed him. The Sioux were taught from childhood to never tell a lie. "I am glad," he said. "I did not want to kill you." He slid the Colt into his holster.

"Where is your horse?"

Eats-With-Bear pointed past the hill. "I hid him and waited for you." He started off but stopped. "How will I speak of you?"

"I am sometimes called He-Who-Walks-Many-Trails."

"I will call you Fast Hands. I saw you shoot the other white." Eats-With-Bear smiled and took a few more steps but once more halted. "Now that we are friends I should tell you of the other one."

"Other one?" Fargo said.

"I was not the only one who followed you from the white village. There was another. I saw him but he did not see me." Eats-With-Bear chuckled in amusement. "Most whites are like rocks. They do not see or hear."

"What did he look like?"

"White," Eats-With-Bear answered in a tone that suggested the question was silly.

"Can you tell me more about him? What did he wear? What was his face like?"

"He had a round hat," Eats-With-Bear said, and imitated the shape by moving his hands around his head in a small circle. "He had a thing here," and he touched the base of his throat, "that was black and like a butterfly's wings." He touched the left side of his chest. "The white man also had a chain, here."

"You don't say," Fargo said in English.

"I do not speak the white tongue."

"Thank you. You have done me a favor."

"There is more. He hid in trees until he saw you were coming close and then he rode away toward the white village."

"It was him I was following."

"Yes. I was to the west of both of you. He never saw me." Eats-With-Bear lifted his hand. "Until our paths cross again." He walked off around the hill.

Fargo reined to the south. It didn't take long to reach the trail to the settlement. The sun was low as Hapgood Pond appeared, the blue of the pond a sharp contrast to the green of the grassland. He swung in at the end of the street and along the buildings to the hitch rail in front of the Blue Heron. Climbing down, he tied the Ovaro off and poked his head in. Milo was at the bar. Maude was at her table, playing her perpetual game of solitaire. Charley Hapgood was gone but several other customers had taken his place.

Fargo moved on to the Sagebrush. He found who he

was looking for. Entering, he went to the bar and leaned on an elbow. "Still here," he said.

Malcolm Keever had been talking to another man. "Why, look who it is. Have you by any chance decided to buy a flask?"

"No," Fargo said. "I came here to talk to you."

Keever motioned at the bartender, who refilled his glass. "About what, might I ask?"

"About why you followed me out to Abe Mitchell's house."

On the verge of tipping the glass to his lips, Keever stiffened. "You must be mistaken. I've been in the settlement all day."

Fargo looked at the man the drummer had been talking to. "Is that true?"

"I wouldn't know. I just got here."

Keever swallowed. "I don't much appreciate being called a liar."

"You were seen," Fargo bluffed, since he couldn't very well produce Eats-With-Bear to prove it.

Setting the glass down, Keever motioned for another. "All right. I admit it. I followed you and the minister out to the Mitchell place. What of it?"

"Why?"

"In my line of work everyone is a potential customer. Abe Mitchell supposedly has a lot of money. I figured to ride out there and try and sell him the most expensive flask on the market. The top half is plated in gold, with a ruby in the center."

"You have one of those flasks with you?"

"No. But I have a catalogue. I could special order it for him at a little extra cost."

Fargo mulled it over. Drummers were notoriously money hungry. The excuse was plausible except for one important detail. "You came back without trying to sell him the flask."

"That's your fault."

"Mine?"

Keever nodded. "I was all set to show myself when

you went and shot that man in the head. It shocked me. I've never seen a man killed before. I was so rattled, I stayed hid and watched the house. I thought there might be more gunplay. Then you came riding out and got close to where I was hid so I got out of there."

"Have any knives on you?"

"I never carry one."

"Mind if I check for myself?"

Keever bristled. "Yes. I've been civil and answered all of your questions but now you will leave me be." He took a step back. "Hold on. It just hit me. Are you accusing me of murdering that poor man the other night? The one I told you about? Tyler?"

"You can prove you didn't?"

"Who do you think you are?" Keever raised his voice in anger. "Coming in here like this and making me out to be a killer. You don't even wear a badge."

Heads were turning. The bartender was coming down the bar. "What's going on here?"

Fargo had two choices. He could pat the drummer down but Keever was bound to resent it and resist. Or he could do what he did, namely, step from the bar and say, "We'll talk more."

"You take too much for granted," Keever snapped.

Reluctantly, Fargo left. He returned to the Blue Heron and claimed a bottle and a corner table. He didn't want company but he got some anyway. "What's on your mind?" he asked as Maude pulled out a chair.

"My, ain't you the prickly cuss?" She placed her deck in front of her.

"Two men tried to kill me today."

"So you act like a stomped snake?" Maude chuckled. "What you need is to relax and I know just the way." She reached over and ran a finger across the back of his hand. "A second helping of me."

"Maybe later on," Fargo said.

Maude began to shuffle the deck. "There's another reason I came over. I heard a rumor today that might interest you."

"Oh?"

She glanced about the room as if afraid of being over-heard. "I heard about you and that lunkhead, Sharpton. Word is that you blew out his wick."

"He asked for it."

"No need to justify what you did," Maude said. "Not to me, anyway. The gents who aim to bury you are another story."

"Where did you hear this?"

"It's all over Hapgood Pond. Rumor has it that a couple of Mitchell's men don't care that he says you are to be left alone. Word is they aim to jump you and pay you back for Sharpton."

"Just what I need." Fargo had hoped that Mitchell had smoothed things over with his gunnies.

"Could be just talk but I figured you should know."

Fargo looked at her. "I'm obliged."

Maude grinned and winked. "I know just how I'd like for you to return the favor."

"This rumor say which two it is?"

"One of them is a man called Weaver."

"I've met him."

"Oh? The other is a pard of his called Hanks."

Fargo downed a third of the bottle, chugging it straight. He was commencing to regret stopping in Hapgood Pond. Had he foreseen what he was in for, he would have pushed straight on.

"One other thing," Maude remarked. "Charley Hapgood wants you to stop by his cabin. He said it was important, said that if you got back late, go right over. He'd leave a lantern in the window."

"Important, huh?" Fargo doubted it. The old drunk wouldn't know important if it bit him on the ass.

"So Charley claimed. But when he's been drinking heavy, he doesn't know half of what he does or says."

Fargo rose and said, "Hold on to my bottle. I'll be back."

"You better. I have an itch you need to scratch."

"My kind of gal." Fargo grinned and walked out into the gray of twilight. The general store was closing for the day and the butcher-barber was in the front window of his shop, untying his apron. Fargo decided to walk to the cabin and left the Ovaro at the hitch rail. The stallion could use the rest and he could stand to stretch his legs. As he moved down the street a vague uneasiness came over him, a feeling he sometimes had when unseen eyes were on him.

He loosened the Colt in its holster.

11

Ducks were paddling about out in the middle of the pond. A pair of geese were honking. Several fish jumped. A startled frog croaked and leaped into the water at Fargo's approach.

Animal tracks were everywhere. Deer, antelope, raccoons, foxes, coyotes, bears, all came to the pond at night to slake their thirst. Near the shore, the water was only a few feet deep. Farther out, Fargo had been told, it was a lot deeper. Exactly how deep, no one knew.

The cabin was small but sturdily built. Clay had been packed between the logs to keep out the wind and the cold. A stack of logs was ready for the fire.

Burlap covered the lone window, which was dark. The door had been made from planks and rattled when Fargo knocked.

There was no response.

Fargo knocked again, louder. Given Charley Hapgood's fondness for liquor, he figured the old man had passed out.

Again there was no reply.

"Hapgood?" Fargo called out. "It's Fargo. Maude said that you wanted to see me."

The cabin stayed quiet and still.

"She said you had something important to tell me," Fargo hollered. "Now open up, will you?" He tried the latch. Leather hinges creaked as the door opened. "Hapgood?" He was beginning to wonder if the old man was even there.

The geese had glided near to shore and were watching him.

Fargo was about to close the door and leave when he saw an overturned chair. Stepping inside, he stopped to let his eyes adjust to the gloom. Gradually shapes materialized; a table a few feet from the chair, a bunk over against a wall, a small stone fireplace and chimney. The place smelled of alcohol and tobacco and the lingering odor of cooked food.

"Charley?"

A lantern hung on a peg on the wall. Taking it down, Fargo lit it and held it over his head. Surprisingly, everything was tidy and clean except for its owner, who lay facedown on the other side of the table, his legs twisted as if he had been trying to turn when he was felled.

Fargo went around the table. He set the lantern down and hunkered. An Arkansas toothpick with a rosewood hilt had been jammed into the back of the old man's neck. A small pool of blood had formed. Fargo touched it and a drop fell from his fingertip. Hapgood hadn't been dead long. Not more than an hour.

He went through Hapgood's pockets and found not quite ten dollars in coins, and replaced them.

Fargo righted the chair and straddled it. He stared at the body, pondering.

"Why would anyone kill you?" he asked out loud. Hapgood had no connection to Abe Mitchell, that he knew of, and all the people murdered so far were either relatives of or worked for Mitchell.

The New Orleans police might be right. The killer might be a lunatic but Fargo doubted it. It had been his experience that people usually had one of three reasons for killing. They killed to slay an enemy, as Eats-With-Bear had tried to do to him. They killed to steal, but the old man had nothing worth taking. Or they killed out of revenge.

Fargo was partial to vengeance in Mitchell's case. It fit the pattern, save for poor Charley Hapgood. The meaning of the knives in the neck eluded him. Maybe there wasn't any. Maybe that was just how the killer liked to kill. It was quick and quiet if the killer had a hand over the mouths of the victims when he stabbed them.

Fargo stood. He picked up the lantern and stepped to the doorway. Night had fallen and stars sparkled in the firmament. He closed the door and bent to examine the ground for tracks.

A revolver cracked and a leaden hornet plucked at Fargo's buckskins. He dived flat as another shot sounded and the lantern exploded in a shower of flame and glass. He felt searing heat in his cheek and the sting of shards. Rolling away from the burning shell, he flattened and palmed the Colt.

The two shots had come from different points. So there were two of them.

The pair Maude had warned him about, he figured: Weaver and Hanks. He snaked toward the far side of the cabin and when he was around the corner rose into a crouch. The shore, as much of it as he could see, was empty, or appeared to be. Either they were flat on their bellies or they were in the woodland that bordered the pond. He bided his time, letting them come to him, but they were too savvy to show themselves. He would have to do this the hard way.

Fargo crept toward the woods. No shots pealed. Tucking his legs, he darted into the brush and went prone behind a cottonwood. The woods were silent except for the wind. He crawled to another tree and on to a third. If they were there they were good at blending in. Damn good.

Fargo was in no hurry to be shot at again. He had the patience of an Apache, and he stayed where he was for the better part of half an hour. Nothing happened. Not so much as a footfall broke the quiet. It mildly surprised him that no one came from the settlement to find out what the shooting was about. Then again, maybe they knew.

Fargo slowly rose. He returned to the cabin and went around it to the water. A frog was croaking. A mosquito buzzed his ear. He swatted at it and went on warily. The pair had been smart. They had tried and missed and gone off to bide their time and try again later. He'd need eyes in the back of his head from here on out.

Fargo swore. He hadn't wanted to get involved, yet here he was, up to his neck in killers. He should light a shuck. He should climb on the Ovaro and ride off and that would be the end of it. But he took it personal when someone tried to kill him. He took it *real* personal.

Voices and laughter came from the saloons. Over twenty people were in the Blue Heron. They stopped whatever they were doing and stared as he shouldered through the batwings. Maude was at the same table and when he went over she gave him his bottle without being asked.

"I heard the shots."

Fargo swallowed and relished the warmth. He swallowed some more. His nerves could use the tonic.

"Your cheek is bleeding."

"Glass," Fargo said, and sank into a chair. He glared at the people staring at him and they stopped staring. "Hapgood is dead."

"Charley? They shot him by mistake?"

"He was stabbed," Fargo enlightened her. "With a toothpick."

"The hell you say." Maude reached over and helped herself to a chug of his whiskey. "Why would anyone want to kill him?"

"You tell me and we'll both know." Fargo took the bottle back.

"Maybe it was done so you'd be blamed," Maude speculated. "Folks have heard that you carry a toothpick of your own." She gnawed on her lip. "Do you reckon it was those two Mitchell men who shot at you?"

"Yes."

"Do you reckon it was them who knifed Charley?"

"No."

"Me either." She helped herself to more of his bottle and smacked her ruby lips loudly. "Damn. This is a fine mess you're in."

"Isn't it, though?" Fargo said.

"What will you do?"

"Try to stay alive."

Just then Quarry and Tamblyn walked into the saloon. They looked around, spotted Fargo, and came over.

Tamblyn doffed his straw skimmer to Maude and said, "How do you do, ma'am."

"Pay me a visit later and I'll tell you," the dove said, and winked.

Quarry had focused on Fargo. "Mr. Mitchell sent us to warn you. Two of the men he hired are missing and he thinks they might be after you. They're names are Hanks and Weaver."

"They were pards of Sharpton's," Tamblyn said.

Fargo sighed and said to Maude, "Better late than never." To the gun hands he said, "I've already made their acquaintance. They tried to bushwhack me a while ago but they are poor shots."

"I wouldn't take them lightly," Quarry said. "They have notches on their six-shooters."

"That lady reverend is looking for you, too," Tamblyn said. "She was upset when you rode off without her."

"We had to escort her in," Quarry mentioned. "She's off looking for lodging for the night."

Fargo had toyed with the notion of spending the night with Maude but now he had other ideas. "Where did you see her last?"

"Heading down the street," Quarry said, and gestured. "The clerk at the general store has a small house and sometimes he and his wife rent out a room at the back."

Fargo rose, pecked Maude on the cheek, and hustled out with the bottle in his hand, saying, "Thanks for the warning." He spied Reverend Honeydew leading her horse down the street. Quickly, he went to the Ovaro and slid the bottle into a saddlebag and then called out to her. She heard him and turned and led the horse back.

"There you are! Thank God. I was worried about you. I prayed you were all right."

"I didn't know you cared," Fargo said, grinning.

"Not in the manner you imply. But I consider you a friend and I care about my friends."

"I have a place for you to stay tonight."

"You do? Where? That would be grand. Mr. Mitchell offered to put me up at his house but I declined. I get the impression some of his men aren't very fond of me."

"They're hired guns," Fargo said.

"So?"

"You're a parson."

"Are you suggesting I remind them of things they would rather not think about?"

"Something like that." Fargo led her to the hitch rail, untied the Ovaro, and headed toward the pond.

"Where is this place you found?"

"You'll see." Fargo probed the night for movement and sounds. Weaver and Hanks were bound to try again. With a little luck, he would make it easy for them. So easy, it would put them in early graves.

"I love it when a man is mysterious," Jasmine said lightly.

"Are ministers supposed to talk like that? Not that I'd fight you off if you had a hankering for my body."

Jasmine snorted. "Tell me. Is that *all* you ever think of? I can't stress enough that I have no interest in that whatsoever." In the pale starlight her face seemed to glow. Her lips, with their natural perpetual pucker, were made for kissing.

"Me either," Fargo said.

"Do you expect me to believe that?"

"It's been a long day. I'm worn out," Fargo fibbed. "All I want is a good night's sleep."

They reached the pond. The ducks and geese were invisible in the ink but he could hear them out there.

"Why have you brought me away from the settlement?" Jasmine asked.

"You wanted a place to stay for the night."

"There's nothing out here except Mr. Hapgood's cabin."

"That's the place."

Jasmine stopped in her tracks and studied him as if trying to read his thoughts. "What are you up to?"

"Not a thing."

"I don't know as I want to stay at Hapgood's cabin. He smells. What does he expect us to pay him for the privilege? I don't have a lot of money with me."

"You won't need any. You get to stay there for free. Hapgood will be gone all night and offered me the use of his place and I'm offering the same to you."

Fargo would tell as many fibs as he needed to persuade her.

"You and me under the same roof?" Jasmine coughed and ran a hand down the front of her dress. "I'm not convinced that would be entirely safe."

Fargo had done enough lying already; one more wouldn't matter. "I promise to behave. But if you want, I'll sleep outside."

"You would do that for me?"

"Anything for a lady."

The cabin was dark, the door still shut. Fargo walked past it and over to a boulder by the lake. "Why don't you have a seat while I air the place out?"

"Is that necessary?" she asked.

"Like you said, old Charley doesn't take many baths. I was here earlier. It smells like a distillery but if you give me a couple of minutes I can fix that." Fargo gave her the Ovaro's reins and went in. The body was where he'd left it. Working rapidly, he turned it over, gripped both wrists and dragged it to the doorway. The reverend was sitting on the boulder and gazing out over the pond. He slipped out, hauling the body, and made it to the woods undetected. He rolled the mortal remains of Charley Hapgood into a patch of high grass and went back in. The bunk had a single blanket. Wadding it up, he placed it on the ring of blood and let the blood soak in. Only a smear was left when he carefully carried the blanket outside and around to the woods and left it with the body. His next step was to move the table over the smear and set the chair where it blocked the smear from view from the doorway. Satisfied, he untied the bottom

85

corners of the burlap and moved the burlap aside to admit the breeze. He let a few minutes go by and went over to the boulder. "All set."

Jasmine raised her lovely face to the stars and breathed deep. "I love it here, don't you? There is so much beauty."

"Yes," Fargo said, running his gaze down her body, "there is."

"Well, shall we?" Jasmine stood, her dress outlining her thighs. "I can't tell you how eager I am to go to bed."

"You and me both," Skye Fargo said.

12

Reverend Honeydew brought in her saddlebags, set them on the table, and sniffed a few times. "It's not as bad as you made it out to be."

Fargo was kindling a fire in the fireplace. Not that they needed one. The night would be warm. He had brought his own saddlebags in and draped them over the chair. The Henry was propped against the wall near the door.

"This bunk, though," Jasmine said, standing over it with her hands on her hips. "It could have lice."

"Wouldn't surprise me," Fargo said. He had secretly hoped she wouldn't want to sleep on it; there wasn't room for two. "You can spread out your blankets over in the corner, there."

"I suppose that's best, although I'm not fond of sleeping on a floor. Still, it's safer in here than sleeping out of doors."

Fargo let her think that. She would be mad if she suspected what he was up to. "How about that flour?" She had mentioned she was hungry and he had offered to make a meal. Between his bundle of pemmican and her flour and salt, he could whip up a tasty stew. She also had biscuits left over from the day before.

"I'll fetch it."

Fargo kept the fire small so she wouldn't notice the bloodstain under the table. He had collected an armful

87

of firewood before coming in, and he added a couple of logs.

"I want to thank you for being so considerate. You can be a gentleman when you try to be."

"Thanks. I think." Fargo got up. She had untied her bedroll and was spreading out her blankets. He went over to help. Kneeling beside her, he grabbed an edge and pulled. Their shoulders brushed. If she noticed, she didn't say anything.

Jasmine sat on the blanket with her hands over her knees and gazed at the crackling flames. "It's cozy in here, don't you think?"

"Cozy," Fargo agreed. He went back out and around the side to their horses. He had picketed both to his picket pin. The saddles were still on. He stripped both animals and carried the saddles inside. It would add to the impression that the reverend and he had settled in for the night.

"I thank you again," Jasmine said. She had produced a hairbrush and was running it through her lustrous curls. "You will make some woman a fine husband someday."

"Like hell," Fargo said.

"You can't tell me you don't like women. I've seen how you look at me."

"When a woman is as gorgeous as you, looking comes easy," Fargo flattered her.

She stopped brushing and pursed her lips. "To be honest, I've never thought of myself as particularly pretty."

"You must need spectacles." Fargo set about preparing the stew. He took his pot and filled it at the lake and set it on the fire to boil. He remembered to retie the burlap so prying eyes couldn't peek in. No sense in being careless.

"I must say, you are quite the homebody."

Fargo almost said that she was the one with the body. Instead he went back out with his coffeepot. Over in the settlement lights blazed and voices and laughter wafted from the saloons. If they were to ask him he would say that he doubted Hapgood Pond would still be there a couple of years from now. It was too close to Sioux territory, for one thing. For another, there wasn't enough graze and tillable land for the ranches and farms the settlement needed to support it.

Fargo hunkered and dipped the coffeepot in the water. The fringing woods were a black wall. Weaver and Hanks could be in there anywhere. He figured they would wait until they were sure he was asleep. He lifted the pot and went through the doorway quickly so he wasn't silhouetted against the light and closed the door after him.

Jasmine was done with her hair. Her legs were straight in front of her and her hands were clasped in her lap. "Tell me about your past," she requested. "I'm curious."

"No."

"Why not? Don't you like to talk about yourself?"

Fargo took the coffee from his saddlebag. "It wouldn't help you understand me any better."

"Is that what I'm trying to do?"

"You're female."

Reverend Honeydew propped her hands behind her and leaned back. It had the effect of swelling her bosom against her dress. "You keep bringing that up. But my being a woman has nothing to do with anything."

Fargo looked at her and deliberately ran his eyes over her body from her hair to the tips of her toes.

Flushing slightly, Jasmine wriggled her legs as if she were angry. "I decided a long time ago that I wouldn't let my gender be a factor in my life. I firmly believe that women can do anything men can do, and often do it better. I chose to be a pastor in part because it is one of the few professions where a woman isn't treated differently than a man."

"Or you picked it because you're afraid," Fargo said.

Reverend Honeydew's eyes flashed. "What do I have to be afraid of?"

"Being female."

"You are suggesting I am uncomfortable with my sex?"

Fargo went over to her. Before she could guess his intent, he bent and cupped her chin and kissed her on the

89

mouth. She stiffened but didn't push him away. Straightening, he said, "Yes."

"You are too bold by half," Jasmine said, her voice huskier. "I'll ask you not to do that again."

"You liked it," Fargo said.

"I did not."

Fargo laughed and carried the coffeepot to the fireplace. He pretended to ignore her. Out of the corner of his eye he saw her touch her mouth and lightly run her fingers over her lips and then angrily jerk her hand down.

"You are insufferable, sir," she declared. "No one has ever treated me the way you do."

"You shouldn't lie."

Jasmine gave a start and said, "Lie about what?"

"As good-looking as you are, men were after you long before you put on that collar. You wear it to keep them at bay."

"You think you know everything."

"I know women." Fargo rose and took his own bedroll and spread his blankets out next to hers. She watched him with visible unease.

"I thought you were going to sleep outside?"

"It's early yet," Fargo said. "After we eat and talk some and you turn in, I'll go out." That much, at least, was true. Or mostly so.

"Oh."

Fargo stretched out on his back with his fingers laced behind his head. The pleasant aromas of the stew and the coffee filled the cabin and made his mouth water. He was more hungry than he thought.

Reverend Honeydew looked at him and looked away. She swallowed and licked her lips and plucked lint from her dress.

"Nervous?" Fargo said.

"I most assuredly am not."

Fargo closed his eyes but not all the way. He shammed resting, and watched her. She stared at his face, then ran her eyes over his body; her gaze lingered below his belt. Inwardly grinning, he yawned and stretched and opened his eyes and sat up. "I almost dozed off."

She said nothing.

The stew was bubbling. He took the pot by the handle and removed it from the fire.

Reverend Honeydew brought over a bowl and a spoon. "That smells delicious."

Fargo ladled some into her bowl and onto his tin plate. He wolfed his portion and ladled out another. By then the coffee was perking and he filled both their cups. They reached for the sugar at the same moment and their fingers rubbed.

"This is nice," Jasmine remarked as she sipped and stared into the fire. "I don't have many peaceful moments like this anymore."

"Why not?" Fargo would have thought that ministers liked a peaceful, quiet life.

"I'll regret confessing this to you, but the truth is, I am constantly at war with myself."

Fargo thought he understood. She was a woman; she had a woman's urges and wants. She was also a minister and must deny them.

"How about you? Do you ever find yourself at odds with what you have to do?"

"No," Fargo said.

"Not ever? What about killing? You shot that man, Sharpton. Doesn't it bother you?"

"Not so I'd lose sleep over it."

"It would bother some people," Jasmine said archly. "Those with a conscience."

"This isn't back east. Out here it is kill or be killed and when someone is out to put windows in my noggin, I put windows in theirs first." Fargo was annoyed that she had brought it up. "Shooting a man who is trying to kill you is no different from shooting a rabid dog that is trying to take a bite out of you."

"Human beings aren't animals."

Fargo sipped coffee instead of replying. It would only provoke an argument and he wanted her in a good mood.

"My parents raised me to respect life. They were very religious. My mother went to church every Sunday and

we always prayed at meals and before she tucked us in."
Jasmine grew downcast and bowed her head. "When she
died I was devastated. Consumption. It was a terrible
way to go. She lingered on and on, to where I wanted to
scream for the suffering she was going through."

"You don't need to talk about it."

"I don't mind. Perhaps it will help you to understand
me. You see, I lost my father a few years after she went.
He died of consumption, too. We lived in Ohio at the
time. Columbus. Ever been there?"

"No."

"It was a nice place to grow up. We had a lot of family
and friends. But after they died I couldn't stay. It was too
painful. So I packed my things and moved off to . . ." She
abruptly stopped and shook her head. "No. You're right.
I shouldn't talk about it. It's too upsetting."

"You can't dwell on death," Fargo advised.

"Sometimes you can't help it. Sometimes the one
who dies means so much to you that it's all you ever
think about. It haunts you to where you aren't yourself
anymore."

Fargo decided to hurry things along. He opened his
other saddlebag and took out the bottle of whiskey.

"Where did you get that?"

"Where do you think?"

"What are you doing with it?"

"Hair of the dog." Fargo added about a thimbleful to
his coffee and put on a show of drinking and smacking
his lips.

"I don't approve of alcohol."

"Try some," Fargo suggested, and waggled the bottle.

"I'd rather not."

"Just a little," Fargo coaxed. "It helps relax you after
a long day. You'll sleep like a baby."

"The Lord knows I could use a good night's rest. But
no, thank you."

Fargo took a gamble. He reached over and poured
some whiskey into her cup and set the bottle down.

"I told you I didn't want any."

Fargo shrugged. "Don't drink it then." It was the moment of truth. Sober, she would never give in. But with a few drinks under her dress, anything was possible.

It took a full ten seconds before Jasmine raised the cup to her ruby lips and sipped. "You know, it's not half bad."

"Have a little more," Fargo said, and added more whiskey.

"Are you trying to get me drunk?"

"I'm just trying to help you get a good night's rest," Fargo said innocently.

"You're very considerate." Jasmine drank and slid back so her back was against the wall. "I shouldn't be so hard on you."

Fargo grinned. He ate more stew while she emptied her cup. He promptly refilled it, putting in more whiskey than coffee. She didn't object. In fact, she downed half the cup in only a few swallows.

"You're right. I'm feeling more relaxed than I've felt in ages."

"Good for you," Fargo said. Good for him, too. He slid closer to her and placed the bottle between them. "Help yourself if you want more."

"I do believe I will." Jasmine added whiskey to the brim. She sat back and sipped and a dreamy expression came over her. "I should do this more often," she said, and giggled.

"It grows on you."

"*You* have grown on me." She giggled louder. "I can't believe I just said that. But you are so devilishly handsome. I've only ever known one man I consider half as handsome as you."

"I am?"

"As if you don't know. I bet the ladies fall over themselves trying to rip your clothes off."

"There have been one or two," Fargo said. "Men would fall over you if you gave them half a chance."

"What makes you think so?"

Fargo put his cup down. He shifted and sat up. He looked into her eyes and said, "This." Then, pulling her to him, he sculpted his mouth to hers.

13

Fargo half expected her to push him away or slap him or at the least call him a beast. But she returned the kiss. Lightly, timidly, but she returned it. She didn't open her mouth to admit his tongue but she did coo nicely when he ran a hand along her arm to her shoulder. She cooed louder when he fastened his lips to her neck.

He nipped her earlobe and she gasped. When he drew back she was breathing heavily.

"I should shoot you for taking liberties."

"You can use my Colt," Fargo said.

Jasmine started to laugh but caught herself and became serious. "Now that you have that out of your system, am I safe in assuming you will stop trying to bed me?"

"Stop?" Fargo kissed her harder. His hands explored her arms and shoulders.

"Mmm," Jasmine said. "You do that well. But enough is enough. I insist that you desist." She reached for her tin cup but he grasped her hand.

"You've had enough."

"I am not a child, thank you very much," Jasmine said peevishly. She pulled her hand free and drank, staring at him over the rim. When she lowered her cup it was empty. "How about more of that marvelous whiskey?"

"You don't need it."

"First you practically force it on me and now you

won't let me have any?" She wagged a finger at him. "You, sir, are fickle."

Fargo didn't think he had given her enough to make her drunk. Then again, if she was one of those who rarely imbibed, it wouldn't take much. "How about if we lie down and rest?"

"How about if we don't?" Jasmine put a hand to her forehead and closed her eyes. "Oh my. I feel so light-headed. Perhaps I should lie down, after all." She eased onto her back and placed her forearm across her forehead. "There. That's a little better."

Fargo rolled onto his side, facing her. Her bosom was rising and falling in gentle rhythm. He kissed her on the lips.

"I like that too much," Jasmine said.

"Enough for me to keep doing it?"

"Hell no," Jasmine retorted, and put her hand over her mouth. "Now look at what I've done, thanks to you and your liquor. I'm not acting as a minister should."

"You're also a woman."

"Stop reminding me. I must be as everyone expects me to be." She placed her hand on her white collar. "That's why I wear this."

Jasmine looked at him and suddenly pressed hard against him, her hot mouth on his. Her lips opened and the tip of her tongue met his tongue. The kiss went on and then she pulled back, her eyes closed, and said, "Damn you."

"We can stop."

"Don't you dare."

Fargo kissed her cheek, her eyebrow, her chin. She looked at him as if she was afraid, then gripped him by the shoulders and fiercely ground against him. Their lips locked. Fargo slid a hand behind her neck. He placed his other hand below her knee. She didn't seem to notice. He caressed from her knee to her ankle and back again. She didn't push him away or hit him so he started to move his hand higher. She immediately broke the kiss.

"No. Please. No more."

Fargo stopped. Despite what she thought, he wouldn't force it on her. "No more," he said.

"Thank you."

In the silence that fell Fargo heard the rasp of the latch. He pushed up off the floor, drawing the Colt, even as the door smashed open. Framed in the doorway was a bearded gunman with a revolver in his hand. They fired at the same instant. Fargo felt a tug on his sleeve. His own slug ripped through the man's gut. The man staggered, swore, and raised his revolver to take aim. Fargo fanned the Colt twice, slapping the hammer as he had practiced countless times. Each shot punched the gunman back another step. The man tried one last time to take deliberate aim, and Fargo shot him in the head.

Instantly, Fargo bounded to the door and slammed it shut. Reverend Honeydew was rising and he shouted at her to stay down. He commenced to reload, his fingers flying.

From outside came a string of curses and then Weaver's voice. "You've killed Hanks, you son of a bitch."

The Colt was ready. Fargo flung the door open and darted outside. The bearded gunman was on his back, eyes wide in the glaze of death. Beyond, a running figure was almost to the woods. Fargo went after him. He snapped off a shot and was fired at. Neither scored. He zigzagged, which lost him some ground, and when he came to the trees the figure was nowhere to be seen. Ducking behind thick brush, Fargo listened. All he heard was the croak of a frog and the chirp of crickets. He glanced back at the dead man. He hadn't expected them to try this soon. All the trouble he had gone to in order to lure them in and they came when he wasn't ready.

The crunch of a foot on a twig caused him to whirl. He came within a hair of squeezing the trigger, and snapped, "Damn it. I told you to stay put." He pulled Reverend Honeydew down beside him.

She had brought the whiskey bottle. "You just killed a man."

"He was trying to kill me. Now hush. The other one is

96

out there yet." Fargo peered into the surrounding darkness.

"Who?" she said much too loudly.

"That man's partner. Weaver is his name."

"Oh. Those two I heard were out to kill you." She giggled. "I wish him luck."

Fargo clamped a hand over her mouth. "Quiet, damn it." He nearly yelped when she bit him, jerked his hand away. "What the hell has gotten into you?"

Jasmine waggled the bottle. "Whiskey."

Fargo fought down an impulse to brain her. He scanned the woods again but he sensed that Weaver was gone. He'd hoped to get both.

"You have to buy another bottle. This one is almost empty."

"You've had enough." Fargo rose and pulled her to her feet. Shielding her with his body, he backed toward the cabin. "If we're shot at, drop to the ground."

"You have a nice behind."

"Oh hell."

"Why are you so grumpy? I'm not grumpy. I feel better than I've felt in years."

Fargo stopped at the body.

Jasmine looked at it and did more giggling. "Doesn't he look silly with his legs out like that and his mouth open?"

"Stand there and don't move." Fargo bent, seized Hanks by the arms, dragged him into the woods next to Charley Hapgood. As he emerged from the trees Jasmine tilted the bottle to her mouth, then shook it and sighed.

"Do you think he'll be upset with me?"

"Who?" Fargo pushed her toward the door while watching behind him. "The dead man?"

"No, silly. God."

"How the hell would I know?" Fargo shoved her inside and followed and slammed the door. Leaning against the wall, he shook his head. "We made it, no thanks to you."

"Grumpy, grumpy, grumpy."

"I should spank you," Fargo said.

"Would you, please?" Jasmine turned and swung her bottom back and forth. "Nice and hard."

"Son of a bitch."

"You should try to go a whole day without swearing. I bet you can't."

She walked to her blanket and plopped down and sat with her hair cascading over her face and shoulders. "I feel so wonderful. Did I tell you it's been years? It changes you, a thing like that."

"What does?"

Jasmine chortled. "Can't say. Don't want him mad at me."

Fargo figured she was talking about God again. "Lie down and get some sleep." He intended to stay up; Weaver might come back.

Jasmine patted the blanket. "Come lie next to me."

"No." Fargo pulled out the chair and sat with his boots on the table and the Colt in his hand.

"I want to do more kissing. I'm not a dove like Maude and I don't have a lot of experience but I think you are a wonderful kisser." She puckered her luscious lips. "Come and taste me."

"Just get some sleep."

"I'm confused. One minute you are pawing me and the next you want nothing to do with me. What's the matter?"

"I was just shot at, remember? I might be shot at again. They came earlier than I thought and I wasn't ready but next time I will be."

"They came earlier?" Jasmine scrunched up her face and her eyes narrowed. She sat like that a while and then said, "It's awful hard for me to think. But if I understand you right, you expected them to try and kill you here. Tonight. At this very cabin."

Fargo nodded.

"But that means . . ." She stopped and her eyes widened. "You son of a bitch."

"Reverends shouldn't cuss."

"I will swear all I want to when I am mad, and I'm

mad as hell. You didn't bring me here so I'd have a roof over my head tonight. You brought me so they would think you were busy with me and would be easy to kill. You used me as bait."

Fargo had to hand it to her. Even drunk she had figured it out.

"Nothing to say?"

"It worked."

Jasmine heaved to her feet. She swayed, then balled her fists and advanced, glowering in anger. "I have half a mind to pummel you."

"Pummel?" Fargo said, and laughed.

"Here I believed you were attracted to me and you were using me. You put my life at risk."

"Simmer down," Fargo said. "You weren't in any danger. They wouldn't shoot a woman." On the frontier the only thing that could get a man hanged quicker was stealing a horse.

"I'll show you calm," Jasmine said, and swung.

Fargo caught her arm and turned her and pulled her onto his lap. He set the Colt on the table and caught her other arm and held her firmly so she couldn't swing again. "I don't blame you for being a little mad."

"A little? I am so mad, I could spit fire. Let me show you just how mad I am."

She kissed him. It was an awkward, wet, sloppy kiss, yet a hungry kiss that went on and on, with her squirming in his lap. He let go of her arms and she roamed her fingers over his neck and shoulders and chest.

"It's been so long," she whispered. "So very long."

Fargo felt himself swelling. He glanced at the window to make sure the burlap was still tied, then at the door to make sure it was shut. Suddenly scooping her into his arms, he carried her around the table and carefully laid her on the blankets. "I'll be right back." He picked up the chair and wedged it against the door so the only way to get inside would be to kick the door in, giving him plenty of warning.

Jasmine impatiently beckoned. The stern, aloof woman of the collar was gone and in her place lay a wanton

Jezebel burning with desire. "Come here," she said throatily.

Fargo placed the Colt on the blanket so it was in easy reach and went to undo his belt buckle. He wasn't fast enough at it to suit her and she moved his hands away and unbuckled the belt herself. She tore at his pants, looked up at him and smiled, and did the last thing he expected her to do: she slid her hand in and gripped his pole.

"Like that, do you?"

Fargo couldn't answer for the lump in his throat. She cupped him and he groaned.

"Like that too?" she teased.

Molten fire spread from Fargo's loins. He mashed against her. It took every ounce of his self-control to stop himself from ripping her dress off. He undid the buttons one by one as he went on kissing and fondling. Finally shedding her dress, he hiked her chemise and savored the sight of her exposed charms. Her breasts were twin globes of perfection, her nipples hard and pert. She had a flat belly and a silken thatch and thighs made for kneading. He couldn't get enough of her and she couldn't get enough of him. Their inner fires became a mutual furnace of raw incendiary lust.

Then he was in her and her legs were wrapped tight around his waist.

He was a steam engine rod and she was velvet and yielding and her soft cries of ecstasy rose to the ceiling beam. He drove into her for so long, he chafed his knees. Suddenly she gripped him and threw back her head and from deep within her rose a long, loud moan of release. She gushed and gushed, her body pumping wildly, lost in the abandonment of her long suppressed need.

As for Fargo, he exploded like a keg of black powder. The cabin blurred and all he heard was the roaring in his veins and all he felt was pure and raw and total pleasure. His tongue cleaved to the roof of his mouth and his body arced as taut as a bow.

Afterward, Fargo lay on his side and listened to her light snores. He pulled his buckskins together and

100

strapped on his gun belt and slid the Colt into his holster. Just in case. He thought about getting up and sitting at the table. He shouldn't fall asleep with the other gunman out there somewhere. But he did. He drifted into a gray cumulous limbo and then knew nothing until the quacking of ducks woke him.

He rose onto his elbows and turned toward Jasmine and was mildly startled to find that she was already up and dressed and sitting there staring at him. "Good morning."

Her hand rose from her side. She was holding his Colt. "Don't 'good morning' me, you cur."

14

Fargo didn't really expect her to use it. Ministers, as a general rule, didn't go around shooting people. Then she thumbed back the hammer. "Put that down. This isn't funny."

"It's not supposed to be." Jasmine's features hardened. "You *used* me last night."

"Only a little."

"I'm not done. Not only did you use me, you seduced me. You got me drunk and took advantage of me."

"It was the other way around," Fargo said. "I got you drunk and you seduced me."

She glared and raised the Colt as if to bash him with it.

"Careful," Fargo cautioned. "That might go off."

"It would serve you right." Jasmine pointed it at him. She was so furious, her hand shook. "I should shoot you but it would spoil my plans. Someone was bound to have seen us come here, and given how gossip spreads, half the settlement must know we spent the night together."

Fargo didn't see what that had to do with anything but if it stopped her from putting lead into him, he would stoke her uncertainty. "Most likely," he said.

Jasmine looked down at herself. "God in heaven. What have I done? How could I let this happen?"

"You're a woman."

She jerked the Colt up and uttered a tiny growl. "Say that one more time. I dare you. I double dare you. Being female had nothing to do with it. I was weak. I drank hard liquor and fornicated."

"It was a nice fornication," Fargo said.

Jasmine half rose and sat back down. She raised the Colt as if to bash him and then pointed it at him as if to shoot him. "You're the most aggravating man I've ever met."

"I'm no different than any other."

"That's where you're wrong," she declared. "Most men wouldn't *dream* of seducing a minister. There are some things that just aren't done and that's at the top of the list."

"At the top of my list is shooting babies."

Jasmine looked up at the ceiling and uttered a short shriek. Suddenly rising, she shoved the Colt at him, and when he took it, she began collecting her blankets and effects, all the while talking nonstop. "This what I get for being stupid. From now on I stick to why I am here. I won't let any man, no matter how handsome he is, distract me. Do you hear me? I was a fool and a hussy. No one will take me seriously unless I take steps to remedy this situation." She whirled on him. "I was never here."

"Then who did I make love to?"

"*I was never here.* If anyone asks, we went for a walk and then I left and you slept in here by yourself." She nodded to herself. "Yes. That's how it was. The sun isn't up yet so if I sneak out now, I'm not liable to be seen. I'll go around the pond and ride into the settlement from the north and no one will be the wiser."

She chortled at how clever she was being.

To Fargo, she was going to a lot of effort for nothing. But if it eased her mind he would play along. "I'll go with you partway," he offered, "in case Weaver is out there."

"You will do no such thing," Jasmine said. "If anyone sees us together this early, they'll know." In a fury she rolled up a blanket and thumped it down on the table. "Besides, that man is after you, not me."

"How about if we get together again tonight?"

Jasmine stopped bundling things and turned, her

mouth open in astonishment. Collecting herself, she said, "Unbelievable. You are the randiest man on the face of the planet. You should have been born a goat."

"We were good together," Fargo said.

Jasmine held up a hand. "No more. Do me a favor and don't say another word until after I am gone. Will you do that much, at least?"

Fargo nodded.

"Thank God." Jasmine hurriedly finished and carried her blankets and saddlebags out. She came back for her saddle and saddle blanket. She didn't look at him, not once. Out she went again.

Fargo heard the creak of leather as she saddled her horse. He let down the hammer on the Colt and slid it into his holster. Standing, he stretched and was moving to the fireplace when she came back in. She walked up to him and extended a finger and he thought she was going to poke him but instead she lightly ran the finger along his chin.

"We *were* good together, weren't we? I won't ever forget you. You have reminded me how . . ." Jasmine stopped and shook her head. "No. I've said too much already." She rose on her toes and kissed him on the cheek. He reached for her but she pushed his hand away and moved to the doorway. "A last word and I'll go. Take my advice and ride out. Don't stay in Hapgood Pond another day."

"There's that other gunman," Fargo said.

"Forget about him. So what if he wants revenge for Sharpton? The important thing is for you to go on living."

"The important thing is to be a man," Fargo said. "And a man doesn't run off with his tail tucked between his legs."

"It's for your own good."

"There's also the knife killer," Fargo mentioned. "Mitchell asked for my help finding who it is."

"What is Abe Mitchell to you? You don't owe him anything. By helping him you might get a knife in the neck. Have you thought about that?"

"I won't turn my back on anyone I don't trust."

"That's not good enough and you know it. Please. For me. I would hate for anything to happen to you." Jasmine smiled sort of wistfully and was gone, closing the door behind her.

Fargo went to the window and untied the burlap. He watched her climb on the sorrel and trot off, her long hair flying, her collar white in the morning gray. He sighed and retied the burlap and set about rekindling the fire and reheating what was left of the coffee and stew. He was in no hurry. He had a lot to sort out in his head.

When the coffee was hot he took his cup and opened the door and stepped out into the chilly early morning air. He stood admiring the sunrise, and drinking. Dawn had always been one of his favorite times of the day. A goose swam by and honked. Sparrows winged out of the woods and flew off to who knew where. Farther down the shore a rabbit hopped to the lake for a drink.

That reminded Fargo. He walked around to the Ovaro, pulled out the picket pin, and took the stallion for water. He was standing with the coffee cup in his right hand and his left hand on his hip when there was a light footstep behind him. He realized the blunder he had made, and spun. But it wasn't the other gunman. "What the hell are you doing here?"

Malcolm Keever was dressed in his bowler and suit, his thumbs hooked in his vest. Smiling, he gestured expansively. "I like to take a morning constitutional."

"A what?"

"A walk. I find it gets the blood flowing and the brain working." Keever gazed happily about, rocking slightly on his boot heels. "I love the water. Always have. It's in my blood, you could say. Just as I warrant the prairie is in yours." He motioned. "Isn't it grand?"

"It's a pond," Fargo said.

"I meant life. We breathe, we have a heart that beats, we eat and drink and laugh and love. We experience the rich headiness of being alive. If that's not grand I don't know what is."

"As fancy as you talk," Fargo remarked, "I bet you could sell a whiskey flask to a teetotaler."

Keever chuckled. "I bet I could, at that. A glib tongue and a quick mind put food in my belly."

The drummer was being so friendly it made Fargo wonder why. "I thought you were mad at me."

"Why? Over what you said about me following you to Mitchell's?" Keever shrugged. "Some of his men came into the settlement last night and let it be known that you are working for him, trying to find out who is to blame for killing that man Tyler."

"And others," Fargo said.

"There have been more?"

"About a dozen. It started in New Orleans."

"You don't say? Whoever is doing it sure gets around." Keever looked at him. "Is that another reason you thought it might be me? Because drummers travel a lot?"

"The notion did occur to me."

"I can see where it would. Personally, I hope you catch the culprit. A person should answer for their misdeeds, I always say."

"Do you?" Fargo said.

Keever breathed deep and smiled. "Well, I should be on my way. To prove there are no hard feelings, look me up later and I will buy you a drink." He strolled off whistling to himself.

Fargo returned to the cabin with the Ovaro. He threw the saddle blanket on and smoothed it. He brought out the saddle, swung it up and over, and bent to the cinch. He got the Henry and shoved it in the saddle scabbard. Next he carried out his saddlebags. He rolled up his bedroll and carried the roll out and tied it on.

Across the pond, the settlement was astir. People were moving about. Milo was out in front of the Blue Heron, cleaning the window.

Fargo went back in. The stew was boiling. He removed the pot from the fireplace and set it down to cool. Refilling his tin cup with coffee, he went to the table and sat. He was at a loss as to what he should do next. He could go around Hapgood Pond asking everyone he saw if they had seen anyone with an Arkansas toothpick. Or he could ride out to Abe Mitchell's and ask Mitchell a few questions.

Then there were the two bodies. He could bury them or he could inform the good people of the settlement and let them tend to the chore. He never had been fond of digging graves.

He had left the door open and could see the Ovaro. When the stallion raised its head and pricked its ears, he set down the tin cup and put his hand on the Colt. The stallion was looking toward the pond, not the woods. He got up and went to the door. A quick glance showed the pair of geese. He shook his head in amusement. "It could at least have been a snake," he said. He turned and carried the pot to the table. He was famished. He ate every last morsel and sat back and contentedly patted his washboard stomach.

He looked outside just as the Ovaro raised its head again. "You're being plumb silly." He was feeling sluggish from the food and the coffee and was tempted to sleep a little. Instead, he gripped the cooking pot handle and went out. He walked to the pond, dipped the pot in, and swirled and rubbed until it was clean.

Turning it over to drain out the water, he walked back to the stallion. The pot fit snugly into a saddlebag.

Only the coffeepot was left. Once he had washed it he would be ready to go.

He went back in.

His back was to the door as he picked the pot up. The rush of footsteps and the stallion's warning whinny were simultaneous. He whirled, and the blade that lanced at his chest struck the coffeepot and glanced off. Malcolm Keever stabbed again, going for the throat. Fargo got the pot up and metal rang on metal. He threw the pot at Keever's face and dropped his hand to the Colt. Before he could draw, Keever lunged and grabbed his wrist. He grabbed Keever's knife arm. Straining, they twisted and heaved, Keever seeking to bury his weapon, him to draw.

The drummer was surprisingly strong. Fargo pivoted and threw his foot behind Keever's leg, attempting to trip him, but Keever nimbly hopped over his boot. In their struggling they turned this way and that and knocked the chair over.

Fargo's boot came down on something underfoot. It was the coffeepot. The pot rolled, and as his leg swept out from under him down he crashed, onto the table. Keever slammed a knee at his groin but struck his leg. He responded in kind, and the drummer grunted and went red in the face but didn't weaken.

Fargo threw all his weight upward. He made it to his feet but Keever slammed him down again. Their faces were inches apart. Fargo butted him, smashing his forehead against Keever's nose. Wet drops spattered his cheeks and Keever cried out and skipped back, swiping with a sleeve at the blood in his eyes. Fargo drew. He had the Colt up and out when Keever's boot caught his wrist. His hand went numb and the Colt went flying. Fargo bent and grabbed the chair and threw it to delay Keever long enough for him to bend and slide the Arkansas toothpick from his ankle sheath. They crouched, and Fargo saw the drummer's knife clearly for the first time. It was a toothpick like his, about the same size but with a rosewood handle.

"I was right about you."

"You know nothing, you damned meddler," Keever snarled. Blood ran from his broken nose down over his mouth and chin. "You have no idea what this is about."

"Tell me," Fargo said. He was stalling while he glanced right and left for the Colt. He figured it must be under the table.

Malcolm Keever opened his mouth as if to answer and then shook his head. "What good would it do? You'd think it was wrong. You'd want to turn me over to that bastard, Mitchell."

"What did he ever do to you?"

"Imagine the worst than can happen to a man."

"Worst how?" Fargo still couldn't locate the Colt.

"Enough talk." Keever adopted the stance of a seasoned knife fighter with his toothpick low in front of him and his other arm chest high. "You shouldn't have gotten involved."

Fargo agreed but didn't say so.

"I don't have any choice," Malcolm Keever said. "You're not part of it but I have to kill you."

"Was Charley Hapgood part of it?"

"He saw my toothpick when I opened my jacket," Keever said. "Or at least I think he did."

"You killed him for that?"

Keever nodded. "And now I'm going to kill you." In a blur of double-edged steel, he attacked.

15

Skye Fargo had a strong dislike for knife fights. They were too fast, too furious, too unpredictable. He had been in more than most men and learned tricks and feints and moves that helped him survive. He needed all of his ability now; Malcolm Keever was damn good with a blade.

It was all Fargo could do to keep from being cut. He dodged, parried, thrust. It didn't help that the cramped confines of the cabin hampered him; there was only so much room. Keever's toothpick swept at his neck and he blocked it with his own. He twisted, shifted, speared at Keever's jugular only to have Keever deftly evade it.

Keever was growing frustrated and it showed. Apparently he wasn't used to someone holding their own against him. He moved faster, an intricate ballet of death that tested Fargo's reflexes. Fargo was cut on the arm and slashed in the side. Neither were deep but that Keever had gotten through his guard did not do much for his confidence.

Fargo spun, slipped a stab, sidestepped. He was breathing heavily and so was the so-called drummer. Keever poised on the balls of his feet to strike. They both heard the clomp of hooves and a voice call out.

"Fargo, you in there?"

Before Fargo could answer, Keever whirled and bolted out the door. The man was as fast on his feet as he was with his hands. Fargo gave chase. As he cleared the doorway he saw Quarry and Tamblyn. Quarry was still on his horse but Tamblyn had swung down and was between Keever and the woods. Keever never slowed; his toothpick gleamed in a lightning arc and Tamblyn cried out. Then Keever was past and flying to the trees. Quarry swore and jerked his pistol and got off a shot but he was too slow. Keever plunged into the undergrowth.

Fargo went after him. He had to end it now or Keever might come after him again later, and he didn't want that. He did not want that at all. Keever flew around a thicket and he did the same, only to draw up short in consternation at the unbroken greenery. He pricked his ears but there were no footfalls, no crackle of brush. To his left was a log big enough to hide behind and he ran to it and warily checked the other side. *Where the hell?* he wondered. He spent a minute searching for sign and finally had to admit that Keever was his match in more ways than one.

Fuming, Fargo returned to the cabin. Quarry was on a knee next to Tamblyn. The straw skimmer lay next to them in a spreading scarlet sheen.

Quarry glanced up and somberly shook his head.

Tamblyn had been cut deep. He was gulping air like a fish out of water, fear in his eyes. He tried to speak but all that came out was blood. Suddenly he shuddered violently, his hand rose toward the sky as if in appeal, and he sucked in a last breath and died.

Quarry slammed the earth with fist. Rising, he growled, "Tell me you got the son of a bitch who did this."

Fargo shook his head. "I couldn't find him."

"You're a scout, aren't you?" Quarry said harshly. "I thought you were supposed to be a good tracker?"

"He didn't leave any sign."

"That was the drummer, wasn't it? I've seen him a few times in the saloons."

"So he claimed."

"How in hell can a drummer get away from a man like you?"

111

"That's what I'd like to know," Fargo said.

"So it was him who stabbed Tyler and has been hounding Mr. Mitchell all this time?" Quarry looked down at Tamblyn. "And now he's killed my pard. What I want to know is why?"

"I have something to show you." He led Quarry to the patch of high grass and the bodies of Charley Hapgood and the dead gunman.

"God Almighty. What are you doing? Starting a collection?"

"The drummer killed Hapgood. Hanks and Weaver tried to gun me and Weaver got away."

"They do that a lot with you, don't they?" Quarry poked the dead gunman with his boot. "Hanks, here, never was very smart. Him and Weaver were pards, like Tamblyn and me." He sadly added, "There sure is a whole heap of killing going on."

Fargo returned to the cabin and found his Colt where he thought it would be under the table. Quarry had followed him. "We should bury them before they get too ripe."

"I know."

Later, as they were digging Tamblyn's grave, Quarry paused to mop his sweaty brow with his sleeve. "What in hell is going on, Fargo? What is this all about?"

"Ask Abe Mitchell."

"He says he doesn't know."

Fargo didn't come out and call Mitchell a liar but that was what he was thinking. All the effort Keever was going to, the things Keever said. There had to be a hell of a good reason for him to follow Mitchell halfway across the continent. As they were tamping down the dirt mounds, he came to a decision.

In the bright sun of the new day, Hapgood Pond was no different from any other settlement. Folks were shopping and gabbing or simply taking a stroll.

Fargo drew rein in front of the Blue Heron. "Treat you to a drink," he offered.

"I'm obliged, but I need to get word to Mr. Mitchell. He'll want to hear about all this right away."

Fargo went in. Milo was at the bar, as usual. There was no sign of Maude.

Fargo bought a bottle and chose a chair at a corner table. He could use a stiff drink. He was on his third swallow when the batwings parted and the last person he wanted to see made a beeline for his corner.

"Good morning, Mr. Fargo," Reverend Honeydew said formally.

"Go away."

"What's the matter with you?" Jasmine sank into the chair across from him. "We parted on friendly terms this morning. Or at least I thought we did."

Fargo was raising the bottle when Weaver came out of the back hall and snapped off a shot. The bottle shattered, spraying Fargo with whiskey and glass. Instinctively, he ducked and drew his Colt, bellowing at the minister, "Get down!" Weaver fired again, the slug digging a furrow in the table. Fargo banged off a shot of his own and Weaver twisted, blood spurting from a shoulder. Backpedaling, Weaver fired three swift shots. When the last boomed Fargo reared up but the gunman had retreated into the hall.

Fargo charged in pursuit. He was sick and tired of this. Almost to the hall, he stopped and peeked around and a shot nearly took his head off. He answered, saw a door slam and then heard the crash of glass. He ran to the same door and flung it open. Cheap curtains were flapping in the breeze that came through the shattered window. He cautiously poked his head out and a slug scoured the wall.

A puff of gun smoke at the back of the saloon gave Fargo a target. Weaver ducked. Throwing a leg over the sill, Fargo hurtled after him.

Empty crates and trash were piled behind the saloons. To the north a bay was galloping off, Weaver hugging the saddle.

Fargo extended the Colt. He took aim and curled his finger to the trigger—just as Weaver went around a cabin. Swearing, Fargo sprinted to the street. Weaver was out of the settlement, his horse flying. Fargo spun and ran to the Ovaro. Vaulting into the saddle, he reined around. *Not this time*, he told himself. He was going to end it one way or another.

Weaver was a good rider, his horse was fast. Fargo was a better rider and the Ovaro was faster. Gradually, he gained. He wasn't in pistol range but it wouldn't be long. The ground was open save for scattered trees and pockets of brush. There was nowhere for Weaver to hide.

The gunman glanced back and did a strange thing: he smiled.

Fargo suspected Weaver was up to something and his hunch was proven right when the earth seemed to swallow Weaver and his horse whole. Fargo slowed and reined to the right but he went only a short way and stopped. Dismounting, he holstered the Colt and yanked the Henry from the scabbard. He levered a round into the chamber and went on in a near-crouch, the rifle stock wedged to his shoulder.

A hat and head popped up. Weaver was looking in the direction they had come.

Fargo dropped low. As lightly as if he were treading on eggshells, he stealthily moved forward. The hat reappeared. He was a lot closer. Carefully parting the grass with the Henry, he saw an ear below the hat. He aligned the sights and began to rise a little higher so he had an unobstructed shot.

Weaver chose that moment to straighten. He spotted the Ovaro and instantly dropped from sight.

Fargo waited. He kept the Henry trained on where Weaver had been. But suddenly the gunman's horse exploded up out of nowhere. Fargo swung the Henry and for a moment thought the horse was riderless. Then he saw a leg and a boot and a forearm wrapped around the horn and knew that Weaver was hanging from the other side.

Fargo could have killed the horse. He could have brought it down with a shot to the head. But he didn't fire. He told himself he would regret it later, and slowly straightened. Weaver didn't swing up until he was well out of range, and when he did, he made a sharp gesture.

"You'll get yours, bastard," Fargo said. He walked a few more yards and solved the riddle of how the gunman had vanished into the earth. There was an old buffalo wallow, plenty deep and plenty wide.

"If I didn't have bad luck I wouldn't have any luck at all," Fargo remarked. Or so it seemed of late. Now he had Weaver and Keever, both, to deal with, and no notion of when or where they would try to take his life.

Disheartened, Fargo returned to the Ovaro. He needed answers and the only one who had them was Abe Mitchell.

Instead of heading south to the settlement he rode to the east. It was pushing noon when he got there.

Several gun hands were lounging on the porch and several more were over by the bunkhouse. None tried to stop him as he climbed the steps and knocked on the front door.

Abe Mitchell opened it himself. "Mr. Fargo! Welcome. Mr. Quarry has told me about poor Mr. Tamblyn and the attempt on your life."

"Attempts," Fargo said.

"More than one? My word. Come in and tell me all about it."

Fargo stepped over the threshold. Farther down stood Blakely, thumbs in his gun belt. They swapped nods.

"Follow me, if you would be so kind. We might as well get comfortable. You must be thirsty after your ride."

"That can wait."

A shaft of sunlight streamed in the parlor window. Mitchell sat on the settee.

Fargo straddled a chair. He folded his arms across the top and placed his chin on them. "I want to know what this is about."

"I told you," Mitchell said politely. "I have no idea."

"You're lying."

Blakely took a step but Mitchell motioned and Blakely went back to leaning against the wall.

"I should be mad but I'm not," Mitchell said. "I can

understand why you must think that. But as God is my witness, I swear to you, I am at a loss. Once it was clear I was being singled out, I racked my brain for an explanation. Now that we know Malcolm Keever is the killer, I'm even more perplexed. I never met the man."

"Not ever?"

"Not in my whole lifetime. I swear."

"Keever never tried to contact you or wrote you a note?"

"There has been nothing in that regard," Mitchell answered. "He just started killing my family and friends."

Fargo wasn't buying it.

"For what it is worth, the New Orleans police thought I was lying, too, and badgered me endlessly. It got so I couldn't go anywhere without them following me and spying on me."

"Have you ever done anything that got *anyone* mad at you?"

"If I did I didn't know it."

Fargo frowned. The man was either the best liar alive or he honestly didn't know. "Hell."

"Frustrating, isn't it? Lord knows, I have spent many a sleepless night wondering what it was about. Trust me when I say I have lived a quiet, unassuming existence. I never offended a soul."

"You had to," Fargo said.

"Perhaps not. As the head of the police force pointed out to me, it could be the work of a deranged mind. Keever might be a lunatic who takes perverse delight in the suffering of others."

Fargo wasn't buying that, either. Nothing Keever had said or done suggested the man was insane.

Mitchell sorrowfully shook his head. "I would give all I have to learn what is behind this. My wife, my son, so many people I loved and cared for, all gone because of this drummer."

"And now he's after me."

Abe Mitchell's shoulders slumped. "I am sorry for bringing this down on you."

"Not as sorry as me."

"Point taken. But I might know a way that we can end the madness once and for all."

"We?" Fargo said.

"I would need your help."

"What do you have in mind?"

"It's simple, really," Mitchell said. "Mr. Keever has already tried to kill you once so it seems entirely likely he will try again. Why he has added you to his list, I have no idea. But I propose we make it easy for him."

"What the hell do you mean?"

Abe Mitchell smiled. "I would like to use you as bait."

16

The night wind keened out of the north. Miles away distant lightning spiked the sky and thunder rumbled. A storm had swept out of the Rockies, but whether it would unleash a tempest on Hapgood Pond or pass it by remained to be seen.

Fargo stood on the south side of the pond and watched vivid bolts cleave the inky heavens. He jammed his hat down against the wind and shifted his attention to the settlement. It was past ten and most of the buildings were dark. Not the saloons; they closed well after midnight.

Fargo avoided looking at the woods. He must do nothing to hint that men were hidden in the trees. Blakely, Quarry, and three more of Mitchell's gunnies were supposed to have snuck in shortly after the sun went down and by now were well concealed. That was the plan Abe Mitchell laid out, and Fargo was counting on Mitchell to hold to it.

He had mixed feelings about being used to lure Malcolm Keever out.

He doubted Keever would be reckless enough to try to kill him two nights in a row. Then again, Keever was a bloodthirsty son of a bitch who had knifed pretty near a dozen people. Maybe he wouldn't be able to resist trying again.

Fargo hoped so. He had an account to settle. It was

another reason he'd agreed when Mitchell proposed that he spend another night in the cabin. So here he was, the wind battering him, a storm crashing far away, the Ovaro picketed and his saddle and effects inside. He turned and went in. The smart thing to do was to prop the chair against the door but he left the chair where it was and went to the fireplace and stirred the beans he had bought at the general store.

Coffee was also brewing. He needed to stay awake and it promised to be a long night. He sat and propped his boots on the table. "How do I get myself into these messes?" he asked the empty air.

He had to chuckle. Here he was being used by Mitchell exactly as he had used Reverend Honeydew.

A rap on the door brought him to his feet with the Colt out and cocked. "Who's there?" he demanded.

"It's me," said a familiar female voice.

Fargo shoved the revolver into his holster and opened the door. "What the hell are you doing here?"

Maude was taken aback. "Is that any way to greet a gal who came out in bad weather to bring you a present?" She grinned and moved her hand from behind her back. "The best red-eye Milo sells."

Fargo accepted the unopened bottle. Under other circumstances he'd have been pleased. "How did you know where to find me?"

"Some of Mitchell's men were in the saloon earlier. They mentioned as how you were staying here." Maude shifted her weight from one foot to the other. "Well? Are you going to let me in or did I walk all this way for nothing?"

"You can come in but you can't stay." Fargo stepped aside and gestured. "Have a seat."

Maude was wearing a red dress and matching red shoes. The dress was so tight it threatened to burst at the seams. She had also done her hair up and reddened her cheeks with rouge. "Why can't I stay if I want? I wasn't planning on going right back."

"I'm expecting someone."

"Oh? Who?"

Could Fargo trust her to keep her mouth shut? All he said was, "Company."

"Maybe I can guess. There's a rumor going around that you and Miss High-and-Mighty have become right friendly." Maude winked and grinned. "A lady of the cloth. Have you no shame?"

"Where did you hear that?" Fargo hadn't told a soul, and Reverend Honeydew wasn't about to boast of their lovemaking.

"I told you. The rumor is all over." Maude leaned against the table and crossed her legs so the dress highlighted the sweep of her thighs. "Tell me it's not true. I gave you credit for better taste."

"She's a woman," Fargo said.

Maude laughed. "I'll be damned. You'll go after anything in petticoats, won't you?"

"You really can't stay," Fargo stressed.

"What's gotten into you? I spread my legs for you, didn't I? Show a little hospitality." Maude moved to the chair. "And close the door. You're letting in a draft."

"Five minutes," Fargo said. "That's all you get." He shut the door and set the bottle on the table. "Help yourself," he said, tapping it.

"I brought it for you." Maude sat with her shoulders thrust back so that her bosom bulged even more and gave him the sort of smile a cat might give a caged canary. "Thought we could have a little fun."

"You're not listening."

"All right, all right. But you did say five minutes." Maude tilted her head and studied him. "What's she like?"

"Who?"

"Don't play innocent, damn you. Who were we just talking about? What is high-and-mighty like with her skirts in the air? Is she half as good as me?"

Thunder boomed, closer than before, delaying Fargo's reply. "A gentleman doesn't talk about a lady behind her back."

"Hell, you're no gentleman. And if she slept with you she's no lady." Maude took the bottle into her lap and

120

opened it. "The next time I see her I'll tell her so to her face."

"I'd be obliged if you didn't," Fargo said.

"It would serve her right. The hypocrite. Why, just yesterday morning she lectured me about the ways of sin. Then she goes and throws herself at you."

"It wasn't like that."

"Whether a woman makes the first move or the man, she's made up her mind before the first move is made."

A bubbling sound drew Fargo to the fireplace. The beans were done. He lifted the pot from the flames and set it down. "Are you hungry? I have more than enough."

"No. I'll watch you." Maude patted the table. "Come and sit with me."

There was only the one chair so Fargo sat near her on the floor. She had splashed on so much perfume that it was like sitting next to a flower bed. "You haven't asked about Charley Hapgood."

"Why should I? I know he's dead. He was a crotchety, smelly drunk who never bought me a drink or paid for a poke. I won't miss him. Nor will anyone else."

"I sort of liked him," Fargo said.

"Next you will get yourself a puppy or a kitten," Maude teased. "You're softer than I imagined."

Fargo elicited a laugh with, "Not where it counts."

The loudest crash of thunder yet quaked the whole cabin. Maude gave a slight start and stared fearfully at the ceiling. "I hope to heaven he built this place better than he dressed himself."

"You're safe enough."

Maude listened, and when a minute went by with only the howl of the wind, she hiked her dress up a few inches and said seductively, "After you're done how about some dessert?"

"You keep forgetting you have five minutes."

"Will you stop bringing that up? I'm not leaving until I'm good and ready and that's final."

"Damn it." Fargo couldn't afford the distraction. "I give my word I'll come see you after this is done with."

"I want it now," Maude said, and playfully wriggled her hips.

Fargo sighed. He filled a bowl with beans and hunkered. "Are you sure you're not hungry? I have enough for both of us."

"No, thanks. I came here to be eaten, not to eat." Maude chortled at her remark, then sobered. "There is something else, though. Weaver has been skulking around the settlement, telling everyone who will listen how he is going to blow out your wick for what you did to Sharpton and his friend Hanks."

"And Mitchell's men didn't do anything?"

"They didn't know he was around. Weaver is real clever about it. He only comes in when they're not there. I didn't hear him, myself, but a friend who did said he is bound and determined to do you in. My friend also said he got the idea Weaver isn't above shooting you in the back. A word to the wise."

"I'm obliged."

"In return I'd like to know why that other man, Keever, is going around knifing folks."

"No one knows."

"Have I mentioned I slept with him?"

Fargo looked up from his beans. "You sure as hell did not."

"Now, now. Don't get mad. I didn't hear tell about him being the knife killer until today. But yes, he paid for a poke the first night he strayed into Hapgood Pond. Or maybe stray isn't the right word since he came here on purpose." Maude pulled at her dress as if to loosen it. "Wasn't much to it. He's not nowhere near as good as you." She smiled and patted both her thighs. "I can't wait to wrap these around you again."

"Keever," Fargo said.

"Well, we made the usual small talk. I asked him what he was doing here and he said as how he goes around selling flasks. I'd never heard of a flask drummer so I got a little interested and asked him how much money he made from it and he answered that he didn't rightly know as he hadn't been selling them long."

"That's all?"

"No. Be patient, will you." Maude grinned and ran the tip of her tongue along her lips.

"And people say that's all *I* ever think about," Fargo muttered.

"Keever asked me if I liked it here and I said as how it was a living and he said as how he didn't like it at all. He wished he was back in the big city—"

"Did he say any city by name?" Fargo interrupted.

"Yes, as a matter of fact. He mentioned New Orleans. And I asked him how come he left if he liked it there so much." Maude paused. "He got a strange look and told me that sometimes people do things they don't want to because they have to. And I said to him, he had come a hell of a long way to sell flasks, and he said that there was more to it than that."

"You didn't ask what he meant by that?"

"Of course I did. As he was dressing. And he got another strange look and said that a man has to live by his principles or he's not much of a man at all."

Fargo stopped eating. "Principles?"

Maude nodded. "Interesting, huh? I was a little curious so I asked him what kind of principles and he said there is only one kind. There is right and there is wrong and a man must decide which he will live by."

"He talks about doing right and goes around killing people?"

"There's more. I joked about him getting all serious all of a sudden and he stared at me and said some things in life are too serious to be taken any other way. That there are losses that run so deep, a person can never forget them."

Fargo was making a habit of repeating what she said. "Losses?"

"I asked if he had lost someone and his face got all dark and ugly and he said that he had and that the man who was to blame would pay for what he had done, would pay as dearly as anyone had ever paid for anything. What do you make of that?" Maude didn't wait for him to reply. "I know what I make of it. There's more

123

to this than meets the eye. Keever isn't just some lunatic, like Mitchell's men are saying."

Fargo had suspected all along that there was more to the murders than Abe Mitchell would admit. Now he was sure of it.

Maude said, "I'd like to talk to Keever some more but no one has seen hide nor hair of him since yesterday. Either he's gone and headed back east or he's lying low. Frankly, I can't see him running off. That look in his eyes—nothing short of dying will stop him."

Fargo agreed. "If he does show up, stay away from him. He's dangerous."

And as deadly with a knife as any man he ever ran across.

"Why, handsome," Maude said gaily. "I didn't know you cared."

"I mean it."

"Why would he harm me? I have nothing to do with Abe Mitchell. Hell, Mitchell has never even paid for a poke."

"Have you heard any rumors about him?"

"Mitchell? His men say he's as nice as can be. He must be awful religious, too."

"Why do you say that?"

"Mitchell doesn't gamble or pay for pokes. What other excuse would a man have for not acting like a man other than religion?"

The pokes part was easy for Fargo to explain. Mitchell was still grieving over his murdered wife and son. As for cards, some men didn't like to fritter their hard-earned money away.

"He does like to drink, though. Fact is, I hear he can't get enough of the stuff."

"He hides it real well," Fargo observed.

"One other thing," Maude said. "Something peculiar happened once."

"Do I have to ask what?" Fargo said when she didn't go on.

"Milo has a wife and daughter, a girl about seven or eight years old. The girl was coming out of the general store one morning just as Abe Mitchell was going in. Mitchell looked at her and started crying."

"In front of everyone?"

Maude nodded. "Blubbered like a baby. His men were downright embarrassed but no one could get him to stop. Milo's wife said he leaned his head against the window and wept and wept. Pitiful, if you ask me."

Again, Fargo thought he knew why. Milo's wife and daughter reminded Mitchell of his own wife and young son.

"What do you make of it all?" Maude asked.

"I don't have the answers yet."

"Maybe you should light a shuck. What did Mitchell ever do for you that you risk getting a knife in the neck?"

"Keever tried once already."

"Exactly my point. Why die for a man you hardly know?"

"It's not for Mitchell. It's for me."

"Fine. Be that way. And when they bury you, don't expect me to put flowers on your grave."

17

By Fargo's internal clock it was pushing midnight. Maude had left hours ago, reluctantly. She had rubbed herself against him and said that he would regret making her leave and he told her that she would regret not leaving if she wound up dead. She'd pouted and he'd smacked her on the fanny and hustled her out.

Fargo was on his tenth or eleventh cup of coffee. He had lost count. He'd had so much, he hardly tasted it when he took another swallow. Setting the cup down, he drummed his fingers on the table and listened to the patter of rain on the roof. So far the rainfall had been light but the wind was picking up and the boom of thunder was near continuous. The storm front would soon arrive.

Fargo wouldn't care to be in the boots of the men out in the trees. They would be soaked and cold before too long.

The burlap flared around the edges with light from a bolt cleaving the sky, and the next moment Nature let loose with a torrent. From the sounds of things, the rain was falling in sheets. A cannonade shook the cabin's walls.

Fargo got up and went to the door. He opened it only a few inches but a blast of wet and wind buffeted him. The rain was so heavy, visibility was a few feet, if that. The drops were big and heavy and pelted the ground like liquid hail. He shut the door and went to the fire-place and added a couple of logs to keep the cabin nice and cozy. As he was straightening there was a light thunk on the door. The rain, he figured, and moved to the table. A louder thunk gave him pause. The rain couldn't cause that. He put his hand on the Colt and stepped back to the door. He was careful and opened it only a crack.

A wet pistol barrel jammed through, the muzzle barely an inch from his left eye.

"You move and you're dead."

Fargo's reflexes were quicker than most but he couldn't dodge a bullet at that range. He stayed still.

"Take one step back and only one step."

Fargo complied. His right hand was still on the Colt and he entertained the notion of drawing if the pistol muzzle wavered. It didn't. The door was pushed wide enough for Malcolm Keever's drenched hat and face and shoulder to poke inside. "Arms out from your sides."

Furious at himself for being taken by surprise, Fargo did as he was instructed.

"Take another step back."

Fargo did.

Keever slipped in and shut the door behind him. His clothes were soaked and drops spattered the floor. "Well, now," he said, and smirked. "Reverend Honey-dew would say the Lord is on my side."

"How do you figure?" Fargo asked.

"The storm," Keever said, and a crack of thunder ac-cented his point. "I know about the men in the woods. I was out there, hid in a thicket waiting for you, when they showed up. I stayed there all this while, wondering how I could get to you with them keeping watch, and then the storm moved in." His smirk widened. "The answer to my prayers, you might say. I crawled right by one of them and he never knew I was there."

"What now?" Fargo asked. As if he couldn't guess. But he wouldn't give up his life without a fight. It just wasn't in him.

"Now we go for a walk. But first . . ." Keever warily sidestepped around behind him and relieved him of the

Colt and the Arkansas toothpick and placed them on the table.

Fargo asked a damn stupid question but he had to know. "You're not going to do it here?"

"You almost sound disappointed," Keever mocked him. "But no. We have a ways to go and something else to do before we get to that, if we do."

"You're not making any sense."

Keever moved to one side, his revolver level at his waist. "First, there's something I need to know. Is it true that you're not on Mitchell's payroll? That you're helping him just because he asked?"

"Where did you hear that?"

"Never you mind. Answer the damn question."

"He's not paying me," Fargo confirmed.

Keever nodded. "Good. Then maybe it will work."

"What will?"

"You'll find out soon enough." Keever reached under his jacket and produced a short length of rope with loops at both ends. "I came prepared," he said. "Turn your back to me and stick your arms behind you, and no tricks."

Keever slid the loops over Fargo's wrists and tightened them, but not to where it hurt. "There. So you'll behave until we have our little talk. We would talk here but one of your friends out in the trees might decide to come in and spoil everything."

"You're going to all this trouble just to talk?"

"You heard me."

"Last night you tried awful hard to stick your knife in me," Fargo reminded him.

"That was then. I've had time to think, and I have a proposition for you." Keever poked him in the back with the muzzle. "Here's how it will be. We're going out the door and around to your horse. I'll help you climb on. Then I'll lead your horse around the pond to where my horse is hid, and we'll head out."

"Where are we going?"

"Somewhere we won't be interrupted. I give you

my word I won't try to kill you if you don't give me trouble."

"Damn, I'm confused," Fargo said.

"You won't be once I've told you what this is all about." Keever stepped to the door and opened it a few inches. Rain and wind blew in, the drops spattering his face. "I hear you like your whiskey," he said unexpectedly.

"You hear a lot."

"True or no?"

"I like it as much as the next man, I reckon," Fargo said. "Why did you bring it up?"

"Because that's your answer."

"What is?"

"Booze. All the people who have died, us standing here now with me holding this gun, it's all because of Monongahela."

"You're not making that up?"

A haunted look came over Malcolm Keever. "I wish to God I was. I wish to God none of this ever happened. But it did and I can't let it be. And maybe with your help I can end it." He pulled on Fargo's arm. "Out the door. So long as you do as I ask, you'll be fine."

If anyone had ever told Fargo that there would come a time when he would want to be led off at gunpoint in the middle of the night with his hands tied, he'd have said they were loco. But God help him, he *did* want to know what in hell was going on. He had been drawn into it against his will and nearly lost his life a couple of times and he damn well wanted to learn why. So he let himself be taken to the Ovaro. The rain was so heavy that he could have darted off and not been caught. But he stayed at Keever's side and let the man give him a boost up.

The flashes of lightning worried Fargo some. It was just possible that one of the gunmen might spot them but no shots or shouts rang out. Keever took the reins, and in a few minutes the cabin was well behind them. Coincidentally, the rain began to taper. The storm front was moving to the east.

Keever's horse was in a stand of cottonwoods. He climbed on and led the Ovaro to the west, out across the rolling prairie. They had gone about half a mile when the rain stopped. Shortly after, so did Keever. He drew rein in the middle of a vast open stretch and announced, "This will do." Then he climbed down and came back and held his hands up.

"No need," Fargo said. He swung his leg over the saddle horn, and dropped lightly to the ground. "But I wouldn't object to you cutting me free."

"Not yet, not until after we've had our talk." Keever moved a few yards away and gazed at a patch of stars that had appeared in an opening in the clouds.

Fargo impatiently waited for him to say something and when he didn't, he prompted him with, "I don't intend to stand here all damn night."

"Sorry," Keever said. "I was remembering." He turned and bowed his head, his hands clasped behind his back. "Where to begin? I suppose with the fact that I'm not a drummer."

"I figured as much."

"What gave me away? I didn't badger you to death like most drummers would do?"

"You're too good with a knife. You had to learn it somewhere and it wasn't selling flasks."

Keever laughed. "You're right. You wouldn't know it to look at me now but I was a river rat once. Does that surprise you?"

"Yes," Fargo admitted. River rats were a tough breed. From the Great Lakes to the Gulf of Mexico, they worked the ships and boats that plied the waterways. Their usual attire consisted of small caps and tight shirts and pants. Their favorite weapon was the knife. Some were partial to big ones, like bowies. Other used dirks and daggers or whatever else struck their lethal fancy, including Arkansas toothpicks.

Keever ran a hand down his suit. "I sure as hell don't look like one now, do I? But I didn't want Mitchell to guess where I'm from."

"New Orleans." As Fargo recollected, the city had

more river rats than just about anywhere except New York.

"The same city as that miserable son of a bitch," Keever said. "I tracked him all this way to finish what I started."

"You admit killing his wife and son?"

Keever looked at him. "It had to be done."

"And you call *him* a son of a bitch?"

"Hear me out before you judge me. A man like you, you should appreciate it."

"A man like me?" Fargo repeated.

"You don't take any guff. You stand up for yourself, like I hear you did when Sharpton and some others were trying to run off the good reverend. Someone does you wrong, you don't turn the other cheek. Am I right?"

"I wouldn't murder a woman and a little boy."

"Oh? What if you had a son of your own? What if you cared for that boy more than you ever cared for anyone? What if he was the apple of your eye and one day he was killed in the most horrible way there is. What if it was Abe Mitchell who killed him?"

Fargo shook his head. "I don't believe it. Mitchell isn't the kind to murder people."

"I didn't say *murder*," Keever replied. "I said *kill*."

"There's a difference?"

Keever gestured savagely. "There sure as hell is. Murder is what I did to his family and kin and friends and workers. Killing is what he did when he ran over my son."

"What are you talking about?"

"You heard me. Abraham Mitchell. He has a problem. He drinks like a fish. He gets so drunk he can't stay on his own two feet. One day he was driving a delivery wagon for that company he ran. He was so booze blind, he ran right over my son. He didn't even try to stop." Keever's voice had grown husky with emotion and he was trembling with the violence of his anger. "He ran over my son and kept on going as if nothing had happened."

"You're sure it was him?"

"I saw it with my own eyes. I saw my son, my wonderful boy, crushed to a pulp with his bones sticking out." Keever sucked in deep breaths and stopped shaking. "I got a good look at the wagon. The name of Mitchell's business was painted on it. I was going to go to the law but what good would that have done? I wasn't rich. Hell, I wasn't even well-off. Not like Mitchell. I couldn't afford a good lawyer. Even if it came to trial, the judge would have thrown it out."

"You don't know that."

"I know there are two sets of laws in this country. One for those like Abe Mitchell and the other for folks like you and me. I made up my mind I wasn't going to let him get away with it. I was going to do to him as he had done to me. I stalked him. Found out where he lived. Saw how happy he was with his wife and son, and wanted to scream."

"You've killed a dozen people to get back at him for accidentally killing one?"

"Haven't you been listening? That one was my *son*. Killing my boy was like killing me only worse because I was still alive. For a long while there, every night I'd curl into a ball and cry myself to sleep, and I'm not ashamed to admit it, either."

"Damn it, Keever."

"I want you to understand. I want you on my side, not his. You are the key to how I can end this."

"Me?"

"You." Keever came a couple of steps closer. "He thinks you are helping him. He'd never suspect if you got word to him that you wanted to meet him. Only when he showed up, we'd spring a surprise."

"That's why you've let me live."

Keever put his hands on Fargo's shoulders. "What do you say? Will you help me see that justice is done? Help me get him away from his gun hands. I'll take care of the rest."

"You *are* loco," Fargo said.

Malcolm Keever took a step back. "I didn't expect

this. Not from you. I thought you would see my side and work with me."

"You've killed a dozen people. One was a little boy."

"So? Why do you keep bringing that up? *He* killed *my* boy." Keever placed his hand on the revolver on his hip. "I don't want to have to do this. What will it be? Will you agree to help me? Yes or no?"

Fully aware of the consequences, Skye Fargo answered, "No."

18

In the dark it was hard to read Malcolm Keever's face. But there was no mistaking his intent as his hand started to rise with the revolver. But he didn't draw. He stopped, and said quietly, "You could have made it easy for me."

"Mitchell has been through enough," Fargo said. "You wiped out his family. Murdered his brother and sister and his mother. Made him run for his life and about ruined him. He doesn't have much money left and nowhere to go."

Keever smiled grimly. "I've done what I set out to do. All that's left now is to finish it. If it wasn't for the gun sharks he's hired, it would already be over."

"What about me?"

"Yes, what about you?" Keever turned his back and gazed across the prairie. "You should have agreed to help me. I'd have let you live." His hand strayed under his jacket and he turned back around.

Fargo kicked him in the balls. Keever cried out and staggered, and Fargo bolted. He ran to the south, bent at the waist and weaving wildly. A shot boomed but missed. It was awkward running with his hands bound behind his back. It didn't help that the grass was wet and the ground slippery and a single misstep would bring him crashing down. Fargo tried not to think about that. When he glanced back he had a twenty yard lead and

Keever was just starting after him, a hand cupped over his crotch.

The ground dipped into a wash. Fargo went down the short slope and up the other side. He nearly lost his footing but made it out and another dozen strides brought him to an area of dirt mounds and dark spots that were holes. A prairie dog town. If he stepped in one of the holes, he'd likely break his leg. He slowed, spotted a mound bigger than the rest, and ran behind it and dropped onto his side. He was breathing heavily and sweating.

Boots thudded. Fargo risked a peek. Malcolm Keever was a darker silhouette against the night.

"Damn it to hell! Where did you get to?"

Keever advanced a few more steps, and halted. "Fargo? I know you can hear me."

The prairie dog town was quiet. No whistling or scampering about. At this time of night the prairie dogs were snug and warm in their burrows.

"Take my advice and stay out of this. I'm going to end it, soon, and then go back home so my wife and I can get on with our lives. Who knows? Maybe I'll have another son someday."

Fargo wished he had his Colt or the Henry.

"I can't drop it. I just can't. I saw my boy die. I saw the wheel go over his small body. I heard him scream. Can you understand what that did to me? Can you understand why I've done what I've done?"

Fargo rolled onto his back, and frowned.

"I'll leave your horse. If you're smart you'll get on him and go. Mitchell's not worth dying for. Believe me."

The night went silent. Fargo raised his head. The silhouette was gone but he stayed where he was. It could be a trick. After about five minutes he rose onto his knees and levered to his feet. He walked north.

Finally he knew what the killing was all about. He felt sorry for Keever. He truly did. For a man to lose his son that way—he could imagine how that might twist someone, how it might turn them into a cold-blooded killer. Revenge was one thing, though; Keever was out to destroy Abe Mitchell completely.

Fargo couldn't muster a lot of sympathy for Mitchell. Not if he really was drunk and driving a wagon. Some stage and transport lines refused to let their drivers drink, with good reason. Mitchell should have known better. But all a drunk ever thought about was the next drink.

Fargo's boots made squishy sounds on the drenched ground. He was glad it was night. In the daytime hostiles were abroad. Now he had to worry only about stumbling on a grizzly—or Keever.

But it wasn't a trick. Fargo walked up to the Ovaro without being shot at. The stallion nuzzled him, and he said, "In a bit, boy." Sitting, he tucked his knees to his chest and raised his backside so he could slide the rope under and out. He had to tug to get it over his boots. His teeth and his fingers made short work of the knots.

Throwing the rope aside, he rose and rubbed his wrists.

It had been a long night so far and it wasn't over. Fargo forked leather and reined toward the settlement. He rode at a walk. A lone light glowing in a window served as a beacon. He avoided the buildings and skirted the pond to the cabin. Wearily dismounting, he faced the woods and called out, "Blakely? Quarry? Are you there?"

No one responded. None of the gun sharks appeared.

The door was shut. Fargo opened it and smiled. His Colt and Henry were still on the table. Then his smile died. He wasn't alone. "What the hell are you doing here?"

Reverend Jasmine Honeydew had pulled the chair over in front of the fireplace and had a blanket around her shoulders. "Is that any way to greet someone who was so worried about you, she came out here in the middle of the night to see if you were all right?"

Fargo checked that the Colt and the Henry were still loaded. He slid the Colt into his holster and leaned the rifle against the table.

"You look a sight," Jasmine said. "Where have you been?"

"Visiting some prairie dogs."

"Don't answer me, then," she said. "I have fresh coffee on if you want some."

Fargo did. He filled his cup and sat on the floor with his back to the wall and grunted with satisfaction at the welcome warmth that spread through his body.

"I needed that."

"I could tell." Jasmine smiled. "I'm glad you're all right. I got here right after the storm ended. Those men startled me half out of my wits."

"Blakely and Quarry and their friends?"

Jasmine nodded. "I knocked on the door and called out your name, and they came charging out of the trees. They couldn't understand where you had gotten to. When they found your revolver and rifle, that quick one, Blakely, suspected foul play. I told him I would stay in case you came back and they went to report to Mr. Mitchell." She paused. "Where *did* you get to, if you don't mind my asking?"

Fargo told her all of it. Every last detail. He drank two cups while he did, and except for his wet buckskins, almost felt like his old self.

"That poor man," Jasmine said.

"Keever or Mitchell?"

"Both, I suppose. They have suffered so much. I will pray for them in the morning. Pray for their very souls."

Fargo rose and began to spread out his bedroll. Dawn was only a couple of hours off.

Bundled in her blanket, Jasmine came over. In a small voice she timidly said, "I can stay the rest of the night if you would like me to."

"I need sleep."

"Oh. Then you don't want to . . . ?" She didn't finish.

"I always want to," Fargo said. "But I have to be out at Abe Mitchell's early." The earlier, the better.

"To tell him about Keever? I'd like to go along."

"What for?"

Jasmine touched her collar. "I'm a minister. I help

people in spiritual need and Abe Mitchell needs comforting if anyone does."

Fargo was too tired to argue. He took off his hat and lay on his side with the Colt in his hand. His buckskins were still wet but he didn't care. "Suit yourself. Be here at first light."

"That will be easy to do since I'm not leaving." She spread her blanket next to his.

Fargo closed his eyes. The heat of the fire and his fatigue soon had him drifting asleep. Right before he went under he had the thought that he was forgetting something important. He was adrift in a black well when a shaking movement woke him. Jasmine was crouched beside him, her hand on his shoulder. "What is it?" he growled.

"Shhhh," she whispered. "I think there is someone outside. I am sure I heard footsteps."

Fargo raised his head. His buckskins were almost dry. Smothering a yawn, he sluggishly sat up. "I don't hear anything."

As if to prove him wrong, the Ovaro whinnied.

In a twinkling Fargo was on his feet and at the door. He pressed his ear to it, then sidled to the burlap and did the same. He heard a faint sound that might or might not be the scrape of a boot. Glancing at Jasmine, he whispered, "Get under the table."

"What on earth for?"

"Do it, damn it." Fargo thumbed back the Colt's hammer and gripped the latch. He was fully awake now, his nerves jangling. Only two people would sneak up on the cabin in the dead of predawn, and both wanted him six feet under.

The Ovaro stamped a hoof.

Fargo flung the door wide and darted out, moving to the right so his back was to the wall. The sky to the east had brightened enough that the surprise on Weaver's face showed. Weaver had his six-shooter out and cocked and he banged off a shot that thudded into the wall at Fargo's elbow. Fargo responded in kind, two swift blasts that raised Weaver onto his boot heels. The gunman didn't go down. He thrust his revolver at Fargo and squeezed the trigger and there was a *click*. A misfire. Weaver pulled back the hammer to shoot again and Fargo shot him in the chest. Weaver tottered. Fargo shot him again, and yet a fourth time, and the gunman sprawled in the mud.

"Finally," Fargo said. He went over and poked the body, then felt for a pulse.

Reverend Honeydew was in the doorway. "Is he dead?"

"Dead enough to bury." Fargo picked up the gunman's revolver. "You have good ears."

"I wasn't asleep. I've been tossing and turning since I laid down." She came out and stared at the body and made a strange comment. "At least this one has nothing to do with Abe Mitchell."

"He worked for Mitchell," Fargo said.

"Yes, but his wanting to kill you had nothing to do with Mitchell running over that little boy." Her voice broke and she looked away and coughed. "Sorry. The thought of it upsets me." She walked toward the pond.

Fargo dragged the body into the trees. He would bury it later. He went back in and added logs to the fire and put the coffee on to reheat. He was rolling up his bedroll when the reverend quietly entered and sat on the chair.

"Do you think it's wrong that you killed that man?"

"It was him or me," Fargo said, annoyed that she would bring it up. "And I'll be damned if it would be me."

"Malcolm Keever and you are a lot alike."

"Like hell we are."

"Please. Be civil and I'll explain." Jasmine slid the blanket from her shoulders to her waist. "Both of you refuse to back down or give up. You knew those two gun hands were after you for killing Mr. Sharpton but you stayed and faced them. Malcolm could have put a stop to his vendetta when Abe Mitchell left New Orleans but he tracked Mitchell all the way here and has his heart set on slaying him."

"Keever said the same thing to me," Fargo said. "And I'll say the same thing to you that I told him." He looked at her. "I don't kill kids and I don't kill women unless they're trying to kill me and I sure as hell don't go around killing someone's mother."

"That aside, I think you have remarkably similar characters."

"You think wrong." Fargo placed his bedroll and saddlebags on the table and poured coffee for himself and for her.

Jasmine was deep in thought. "It's amazing, isn't it, the things people will do in the name of love? Malcolm never killed anyone in his whole life until his son was taken from him. The loss turned him from a loving father into a hunter of men."

"You talk as if you really know him."

"I did, in fact, have a conversation with him the first evening I arrived," she replied. "I got to know him very well."

"Sure you did." Fargo squatted close to the fire to dry his buckskins the rest of the way. He barely listened as she prattled on about honor and devotion until she made a remark that irritated him.

"I respect Malcolm Keever. Anyone who has ever lost a child through the neglect or stupidity of others would respect him, too."

"Isn't there something in that Bible you admire about thou shall not kill?" Fargo sarcastically asked.

Reverend Honeydew colored pink. "Point taken. I was only making my feelings clear. I won't mention it again."

"Good."

The ground was soft from the rain. Digging a shallow grave didn't take long. Fargo packed the dirt down by tramping on it and got his boots so muddy that he walked to the lake and dipped first one foot and then the other in the water to clean the mud off.

The reverend's horse was in Hapgood Pond. She had left it saddled at a hitch rail, and she made a face when he helped her mount. "It's still wet and slippery. What if I fall off?"

"The ground will catch you," Fargo said.

By then the sun was up and Milo was coming down the street. He opened the Blue Heron.

Fargo was a few steps behind the bartender as he crossed to the bar. Milo heard him, and stopped.

"It's early yet. Come back in an hour and I'll be ready for business."

"A bottle," Fargo said.

"For breakfast? Damn, man." Milo shook his head. "You'll drink yourself into an early grave."

"It's not for me. It's for someone else."

"Who?"

Fargo motioned at the shelf and Milo went around and set a bottle on the bar.

"Here you go. I hope whoever you are buying it for appreciates it."

"He won't," Fargo said.

19

The morning sun turned the gray of the house almost yellow. Several of the gun hands were on the porch, Quarry among them. He greeted Fargo with a smile and looked quizzically at the bottle.

"Is he up?" Fargo asked.

"Mr. Mitchell? He rises with the sun. I'll tell him you're here."

"Don't bother." Fargo marched on in. He went down the hall to the parlor. It was empty. Low voices from the kitchen told him where they were.

Abe Mitchell was at the table, stirring tea in a china cup. A tea kettle sat on the stove. "Mr. Fargo!" he exclaimed. "This is a surprise."

Blakely had been leaning against the wall and as Fargo came in he flashed his hand to his revolver. "What are you doing here?"

Fargo stepped to the table and smacked the bottle down next to the china cup. "Drink," he said.

Abe Mitchell's brow creased and he half smiled as if it were some kind of joke. "I'm sorry?"

"Drink," Fargo said again. "I'll make it easy for you." He opened the bottle and put it back down.

Blakely took a step away from the wall. "What the hell are you doing?"

The minister and Quarry came in.

Mitchell smiled at her and said, "Good morning, Reverend. Perhaps you can tell me what this is about?"

"I'd rather let Mr. Fargo explain."

"Explain what?"

Fargo leaned on the table. "Is it true?"

"Is what true?"

Fargo grabbed the bottle and shoved it under Abe Mitchell's nose. Mitchell recoiled as if it were poison, put a hand over his nose and mouth, and shook his head.

"Don't. Please."

"What can a little coffin varnish hurt?" Fargo asked almost savagely. "Have a spoonful with your tea."

"Oh God." Mitchell clutched his arms to his chest. "Get it away from me. The smell is more than I can bear."

"What the hell is going on?" Blakely demanded. He looked as confused as he sounded.

"Please," Mitchell pleaded. "I don't dare have so much as a drop. If I do, I won't be able to stop." His eyes watered and his throat bobbed. "I have a drinking problem. I've had it for years."

"You had it when you ran over that little boy."

"What?" Blakely and Quarry both said at the same time.

Mitchell became as pale as paper and broke out in a sweat. He uttered a tiny sob and lowered his forehead to the table, nearly spilling the tea. "Oh God, oh God, oh God."

Fargo smacked the table. "You lied to me, you son of a bitch. You knew all along what this was about. All the people who have died was on account of *you*."

Mitchell raised a face twisted by sorrow. Tears trickled down his cheeks, and he had to cough before he could speak. "Yes, I've always known. I never told anyone but there was a note beside my son's body. It read, *An eye for an eye, a boy for a boy*. My wife and son and my mother and all those others were murdered because of a little boy who ran out in front of me."

"You didn't stop after you ran over him?"

Mitchell whimpered. "I panicked. I didn't see anyone else so I lashed the team. I thought I got away unseen."

Reverend Honeydew was aghast. "Dear Lord. You don't mean to say you never checked to see if the boy was still alive?"

Mitchell shook his head. "I was too scared."

"You were too drunk," Fargo said.

"Yes, I had been drinking," Mitchell confessed. "I drank all the time back then. It was the pressure. My wife wanted a nice house and nice things and I had to work myself to the bone to make ends meet. I even took the wagon to the docks now and then since it was less I had to pay the drivers."

"You didn't show the note to the police?" Reverend Honeydew asked.

"No. I would have to tell them what it was about. Everyone would have learned about the boy I ran over." Mitchell sniffled and ran a sleeve across his nose. "I never could understand that part," he said, more to himself than to them.

"What part?" Fargo said.

"The boy. There was never any mention of it in the newspapers. Nothing at all. I thought that maybe he hadn't been badly hurt. That I only thought my wheel ran over him." Mitchell looked up. "Don't you see? Until I read that note I thought I only imagined the bump as the wheel went over him. I thought it was the alcohol."

"God in heaven," Jasmine quietly breathed.

"You killed a kid?" Quarry said.

"And the boy's parents have been out to destroy me ever since," Mitchell forlornly replied. "They weren't content with murdering my wife and son. They had to go after the rest of my family and those who worked for me."

"They wanted you to suffer for what you had done," Jasmine observed.

"They?" Fargo said. "Unless Malcolm Keever has his wife hid off in the hills somewhere, he's here alone."

Blakely had been listening intently. Now he put a hand on Mitchell and said, "I don't care what this is about. You hired me to protect you and that's what I'll do. This Keever shows his face, I'll shoot it off."

"Thank you," Mitchell said.

"Maybe you don't care," Fargo said to the quick-draw artist. "But I'm through." He refused to help a man who had lied to him and who was a coward, to boot.

"I'll pay you," Abe Mitchell said.

"Go to hell." Fargo grabbed the bottle, wheeled, and strode out to the front porch. He'd had his fill of Hapgood Pond. It was high time he rode on.

He took a swallow, shoved the bottle at a surprised gun hand, and went down the steps to the Ovaro. He was reaching for the saddle horn when the screen door banged.

"You're leaving without saying good-bye?"

"I have somewhere to be." The saddle creaked under him, and Fargo was up.

Reverend Honeydew was unhappy. "So you told me. I just thought . . ." She came down and put a hand on his stirrup. "A simple hug would have been nice."

"Good luck to you," Fargo said. He raised the reins but she didn't move.

"You don't fool me. You're not as hard as you make yourself out to be. Not like Malcolm Keever. He's obsessed. He won't be happy until Abe Mitchell is dead."

"Not my problem," Fargo said curtly.

"No, it's not." Jasmine stepped back, and smiled. "I want to thank you. You've reminded me of what it's like. A man and a woman, together. I'd almost forgotten, it's been so long since my life was any semblance of normal."

"You chose to wear that collar. No one forced you."

"Huh? Oh. Yes. I did." Jasmine ran her finger along it. "People wear many costumes in a lifetime, don't they?"

"I wear these," Fargo said, and touched his buckskins. He nodded at her and tapped his spurs. It felt good to be under way. He never should have stayed on in the first place. If experience had taught him anything, it was to fight shy of situations like this unless he had a damn good reason to get involved.

A vast vista of prairie stretched before him. The land had been washed clean by the rain and it was a beautiful day. Birds were singing and butterflies were flitting about.

Fargo was almost out of sight of the house when he glanced back for a last look. He heard the thud of boots and shifted toward a gully he was passing just as iron hands seized his leg and he was bodily wrenched loose of the saddle and upended. He clutched at the saddle horn but missed. Down he tumbled, and hit hard on his shoulder. It sent pain clear down his back. He rolled and his hat fell off. Pushing onto his hands and knees, he stared up into the flinty eyes of Malcolm Keever.

Keever drew his rosewood-handled Arkansas toothpick. "I'm going to do this quiet so they don't hear."

"I was leaving," Fargo said. "I wanted no more part of this."

"Bullshit. You were hunting for me." Keever crouched. "Get up. I owe you, now, too."

"You're making a mistake," Fargo said. His hand found his ankle sheath and he palmed his own toothpick.

"I found out what you did, you son of a bitch. You're the one who made the mistake."

"You mean in offering to help Mitchell?"

"Play innocent. That's not what I'm talking about and you know it." Keever moved his toothpick in small circles. "I want you in pain when you die. I want you to beg and plead and cry."

"It will be a cold day in hell when I blubber like a baby."

"We'll see," Keever confidently declared, and waded in swinging.

Fargo was forced to give way. That he wasn't cut was a wonder. Keever was possibly the best knife fighter he ever faced. He parried, twisted, countered, thrust. He stabbed high. He stabbed low. They were so evenly matched that neither could get through the other's guard. Circling, feinting, lunging, they were constantly in motion. Blade pinged on blade, and then Fargo felt a sharp sting in his left forearm. Keever smiled. He knew he had scored. It emboldened him to press in harder. Fargo was bleeding but not badly. He held his own, reacting and acting purely on instinct and reflex. The other's cold steel missed his neck by a whisker. He sliced into Keever's shoulder. The rose-handled toothpick speared at his stomach and he shifted and thrust his own toothpick up and in under Keever's ribs.

Malcolm Keever stiffened and gasped. He took several steps back, scarlet beginning to stain his shirt. He looked down at himself and said in shock, "No. Not like this."

Fargo balanced on the balls of his feet, his toothpick dripping blood. "You brought it on yourself, you stupid bastard." He was good and mad. "I told you I was leaving."

"I should have just shot you," Keever said.

"Your killing days are over."

The stain had spread to all of Keever's middle and the top of his pants. He teetered, righted himself, and his arms drooped to his sides. He gazed toward Mitchell's house and tears filled his eyes. "Now it won't be me."

Fargo stayed ready. He wasn't taking any chances. "All the trouble you went to, and for what?"

"It wasn't for nothing. His wife is dead. His son. His brothers. His sister. His mother. His business was ruined, and he had to run for his life."

"That wasn't enough for you, was it?"

"No," Keever admitted. "There could never be enough. Even killing him won't be." Keever looked at Fargo. "Unless you've lost a son you could never understand." He swayed and almost fell.

"It won't be long," Fargo said.

"No, it won't." Keever dropped his toothpick and sank to his knees with his hands on his belly. He groaned and said through clenched teeth, "You're one tough son of a bitch."

"I hope it hurts."

"It does." Keever coughed, and blood flecked his lips "Do me a favor."

"No."

"Ask that reverend to say a few words over me. Have her pray for my soul and give me her blessing."

"As if that will do you any good."

"One more thing," Keever said. "Have them bury me with my knife."

"You sick bastard."

"I am a father who lost a son," Malcolm Keever said, and died. His eyes rolled up in their sockets and he plopped to the earth and went limp.

Frowning, Fargo straightened. He wiped his toothpick clean on Keever's jacket and replaced it in his ankle sheath. Hiking his sleeve, he examined the cut. It had already stopped bleeding. "I was damn lucky," he said to himself.

The Ovaro hadn't gone far. Fargo hoisted the body over the saddle, stuck the rosewood-handled toothpick under his belt, and headed back. The beauty had gone out of the day. He didn't hear the birds or see the butterflies.

When he came around the corner of the house to the front porch, Quarry took one look and ran inside. Gunmen came hurrying from the bunkhouse. No one said anything.

Abe Mitchell and Blakely and Reverend Honeydew filed out. Delight and relief lit Mitchell's face, and he blurted, "Can it really be?"

Fargo dumped the body on the ground. "It's over."

"Thank God!"

Reverend Honeydew came off the porch. She looked down at the mortal remains of Malcolm Keever and said sadly, "Ashes to ashes, dust to dust."

Fargo handed her Keever's toothpick. "He wanted to be buried with this."

He decided to tell her the rest. "He also wanted you to say a few words over him when they put him under."

"I will see that it's done right," she said.

Fargo swung onto the Ovaro and lifted the reins. He felt bitter through and through. "Damn, I could use a drink."

Abe Mitchell was beaming. "Climb back down and

148

you can have all you want. I wouldn't mind getting drunk myself."

"I bet you wouldn't," Fargo said in disgust. He reined around and said in parting, "I want nothing more to do with you, mister."

"Why are you so upset with me?" Mitchell asked. "He was a rabid killer. He deserved what he got."

"Deserve has nothing to do with it," Fargo said angrily. "If it did, you would be lying there next to him." He touched his hat to the reverend and gigged the Ovaro and rode around the house and off across the prairie, and this time he didn't look back.

20

It was two days later, early in the morning, that Fargo spotted smoke ahead, along the same stream he was following. He shucked the Henry and approached with caution. In a small clearing stood a mule. On a log beside the fire sat an elderly man dressed all in black, wearing a flat-brimmed hat with a round crown. Fargo brought the Ovaro out into the clearing and the man looked up at him and smiled a friendly smile. Around the man's neck was a white collar. "Oh, hell," Fargo said.

The man laughed. "I work for the other place." He rose and offered a strong hand. "How do you do? Pastor Greeley is what they call me. You're welcome to share whatever I have that you might need."

"Thicker than flies," Fargo said.

"I beg your pardon?"

Fargo dismounted and shook his head in amusement. "You are the second Bible-thumper I have run into in a week."

"Is that so?" Pastor Greeley reclaimed his log. "I didn't realize another man of the cloth was in this territory. But then, I am a Baptist, and who knows what those pesky Catholics and Methodists and Presbyterians are up to."

He chuckled as he said it.

"It wasn't a man. It was a woman."

"Pardon?"

"A woman preacher. Or don't you Baptists have those?"

"Son, I've only ever heard of one woman having a license to preach, and the last I heard, she was tending to a flock in Boston."

Fargo wasn't sure he had heard correctly. "You have to have a license to talk about God?"

"Of course. We can't have just anybody going around spreading the Word." Pastor Greeley leaned forward. "But tell me more about the woman you met. I'm most curious. Which denomination is she with?"

Fargo shrugged. "I didn't pay a whole lot of attention."

"Surely she mentioned it."

It took a bit for Fargo to recollect. "The Congregational Church, she said it was."

"No!" Pastor Greeley declared.

"She bragged as how they have been ordaining women for years." Fargo remembered something else. "And they have twenty or more female preachers running around."

"How strange."

"She has a collar like yours and is always saying how we all need to get along."

"How very strange."

The preacher seemed so troubled that Fargo asked, "Why do you look as if you're trying to lay an egg?"

"I must confess to being confused," Greeley said. "I simply don't see how what you say can be true."

Now it was Fargo who said, "Pardon?"

"Well, to start with, the Congregational Church has only ever ordained one woman that I know of. The woman I was telling you about, in Boston. Her name is Antoinette Brown. I've never heard her preach but I hear she is marvelous. A real firebrand."

"Only one?"

Pastor Greeley nodded. "It made the newspapers. There was considerable controversy. She went to Oberlin College, you see, and . . ."

Fargo interrupted with, "That's the same college the female reverend mentioned."

"How very curious. Antoinette Brown is the only female they ever admitted to their theology course. Even then, they let her sit in on the courses but refused to give her a degree."

"The only one?" Fargo said.

"So far as I know. I could be mistaken but I try to keep up with the latest news regarding matters of faith." Greeley smiled. "Perhaps you misunderstood and she was talking about Antoinette Brown and not herself."

"No," Fargo said. "It was her."

"I just don't see how that can be." Greeley sat up. "But where are my manners? Would you care for a cup of coffee?"

"Much obliged." Fargo accepted it and sat listening with half an ear as the preacher talked about how he had received a calling from God to come minister to those on the frontier in need of what the preacher called "spiritual sustenance."

When Greeley paused to take a breath, Fargo asked, "Are you sure about that Brown woman?"

"I read the articles," the pastor said. "I have talked to people who have heard her give sermons."

Fargo downed the rest of the coffee in a couple of gulps, handed the cup back, and stood.

"Leaving so soon?"

Fargo gazed to the west. "Two damn days," he said.

"I'm sorry?"

"Have you ever been played for a jackass, Parson?"

"Not that I know of. If anything, people tend to show more respect for me because of my collar."

"They trust you more," Fargo said. "They let you into their homes and never suspect you would stab them in the back."

"What a peculiar thing to say."

Fargo turned to the Ovaro. "I have to go." He grabbed the reins and went to climb on.

Pastor Greeley stood. "Are you riding to see that female preacher you told me about?"

"I surely am." Fargo hoped he was wrong but if Greeley was right, then he had been the biggest fool this side of creation.

"I'd very much like to go with you and meet her," the pastor requested.

Fargo hesitated. He had a lot of hard riding to do.

"Please. I promise not to be a burden. I can tell you are anxious, and my mule can go all day without tiring."

"Can he go all day *and* all night?" Fargo asked.

"You really are anxious, aren't you?" Greeley rubbed his chin. "But very well. All day and all night it is, and if I can't keep up, then you just go on without me."

The mule proved as good as the pastor's word. Both animals were lathered with sweat and Fargo was weary to the bone when the gray house loomed in the early dawn light. None of the windows were aglow. The bunkhouse was dark, too.

Fargo drew rein and stepped up onto the porch and raised his fist to knock.

The door was open a few inches.

Fargo drew his Colt and pushed the door all the way with his foot. The hall beyond was as black as pitch.

Pastor Greeley had climbed down and was stiffly stretching. "Why do you need your gun? Whose home is this? Not yours, I take it?"

"You'd best stay out here," Fargo suggested.

"Nonsense. I'm not afraid."

The skin on his back prickling, Fargo stepped over the threshold. The silence of a tomb prevailed. "Mitchell!" he hollered. "Abe Mitchell! Are you in here?"

"What is that smell?"

Fargo had caught the odor, too. The odor of the fruit of lies and deceit. "Son of a bitch."

"You swear a lot," Pastor Greeley said.

The parlor was empty. The same with the kitchen. The smell was stronger at the bottom of the stairs, stronger still at the top.

Abraham Mitchell was on his back in bed, wearing a nightshirt so soaked with blood that it was more red than white. His throat had been slit from ear to ear.

His glazed eyes were wide open in surprise, suggesting to Fargo that Mitchell woke up as the rosewood-handled toothpick was slicing his jugular.

"My God." Pastor Greeley had both hands over the lower half of his face. "Is that the man named Mitchell you told me about?"

Fargo grimly nodded. He checked the other rooms but Mitchell was the only one in the house. Scarcely breathing, he hurried down and out and stood on the porch sucking in great lungfuls of clean air.

"That was awful." The pastor leaned on the rail, his complexion almost as gray as the house. "Who could do such a terrible thing?"

Fargo crossed to the bunkhouse. The bunks had been stripped of their sheets and blankets. Other than furniture—the bunks and a table and chairs—the place was empty.

Pastor Greeley had followed him. "Where did everyone get to?"

"Mitchell figured he didn't need his gun hands anymore. The person he thought was out to kill him was dead so he paid them off and sent them on their way." Or so Fargo guessed. "He was all alone when the end came."

"You didn't answer me. Who could have done such a gruesome deed?"

"A woman of the cloth," Fargo said.

"I refuse to believe that. No minister of the Lord could be so vicious. Not if they live true to the Word of God."

"What is the truth?" Fargo said. He wheeled and made for the Ovaro. "I'd be obliged if you would see to the burying."

The pastor was hard pressed to match his stride. "You can count on me. I will send him to his reward." He paused. "Is there anything special you would like me to say over the grave?"

"Here lies an idiot." Fargo stepped into the stirrups and reined to the west. The Ovaro was worn from the long days of riding so he held to a walk. There was no need for haste. Either she was there or she wasn't.

Hapgood Pond might as well be a cemetery. Only a

few people were out and about. A horse was tied to the hitch rail in front of the Blue Heron. Fargo brought the Ovaro to a stop next to it and stared at the animal with regret in his eyes.

Milo was tending bar. Two men were nursing drinks and two others were playing dice.

Maude was at her usual table, playing her usual solitaire. "Skye!" She squealed in delight and rose and hugged him to her abundant bosom. "You came back. Don't tell me you missed me?"

"Where is she?" Fargo asked.

"Who?" Maude said, then added, "Oh. You won't believe it. She marched in here the morning after you left. Took off that white collar of hers and announced that she was giving up being a minister."

"What do you know?"

"It sure surprised me," Maude said. "But what she did next surprised me even more. She paid for a bottle and sat at a table and drank the whole damn thing at one sitting. She's been here since."

"Where?"

"She took a room in the back. She'll come out, drink some more, and go back and sleep it off. What do you make of it?"

"Any sign of Blakely or Quarry or the others?"

"They showed up early in the evening about four days ago. Mr. Mitchell had paid their wages and they were heading off to look for new work."

"When was the last time you saw Mitchell?"

Maude shrugged. "Before you lit out. But he never does come into the settlement all that much."

"And he won't ever again." Fargo put his hand on his Colt and stepped to the hallway. "Which room?" he asked over his shoulder.

"The last one on the right." Maude took a few steps. "What's going on, anyway?"

"Stay here."

The hall was dark, the door in shadow. Fargo stayed clear of it and knocked. When there was no answer he knocked again, louder.

"Who is it?" came a muffled voice.

The door wasn't bolted.

Jasmine was on the bed, bundled in blankets. Her hair was a mess and she looked like hell. On the floor were several empty whiskey bottles. He kicked one and it clattered across the floor and struck the wall. "You should have kept going."

Holding a blanket in front of her, she rose onto her elbows. "I didn't expect to ever see you again."

Fargo stood at the foot of the bed. "So which is it? His wife? His sister? A friend?"

"Wife," she said.

"Is Jasmine even your real name?"

"As a matter of fact, it is. Jasmine Keever." She rose higher, her back against the wall. "How did you catch on?"

"I ran into a real parson."

"What now?" she asked. "Do you avenge Abe Mitchell like I avenged my son?"

"You're forgetting your husband."

"Not ever," Jasmine said. "I loved Malcolm. He worked hard and treated me and our boy nice."

"You loved him so much, you slept with me," Fargo said.

"Neither of us were saints. And I can't help it you're so damn handsome."

Jasmine fussed with her hair with her left hand but her right stayed under the blanket. "Malcolm fooled around a little so why couldn't I? That doesn't mean we loved our son any less."

"Whose idea was it for him to pretend to be a drummer and you to pretend to be a preacher?"

"Mine. We were pretty good at it, don't you think?"

"You had me fooled." Fargo took his hand off the Colt. "That's all I wanted to know." He turned toward the doorway.

"You're leaving?"

"Yes."

"Just like that?"

"I'm not the law. You got away with it. There's nothing I can do even if I wanted, and I don't."

"You could tell a federal marshal. All those people in New Orleans—I killed some of them. I'd be thrown in prison for the rest of my life."

"I won't tell," Fargo said.

"I wish I could believe you." Jasmine swept her right hand from under the blanket. She was holding a revolver and cocked it as she pointed it at him. "I'm sorry but I can't let you live."

Fargo drew and fired from the hip. His slug caught her just above the nose and smashed her head against the wall. There were no convulsions, no outcries. She sank down and was still.

Fargo scowled and shoved his smoking Colt into his holster. Everyone looked at him when he strode out into the saloon. He went straight to the bar. "A bottle," he growled.

"What happened back there?" Maude asked. "Where's Reverend Honeydew?"

Skye Fargo let the whiskey burn his throat before he answered. "In hell, where she belongs."

LOOKING FORWARD!

**The following is the opening
section of the next novel in the exciting
Trailsman series from Signet:**

TRAILSMAN #348
BACKWOODS BRAWL

*Northeast Arkansas, 1860—where the hunter
quickly becomes the hunted, and Skye Fargo
discovers that a fish rots from the top.*

Skye Fargo's Ovaro stallion gave a soft whinny from the
stand of pines where Fargo had tethered him.

A *whinny*, Fargo reminded himself, not a trouble
whicker. And a soft whinny, at that—the kind he gave
Fargo when greeting him in the morning.

Even so, Fargo felt a little tingle of unease.

But the man some called the Trailsman hated like
hell to think about stirring his stumps right now. He was
sprawled fully clothed in buckskins, up to his neck in
the quick-flowing water of a clear sand-bottom creek in
northwest Arkansas. The fast current was rinsing some
of the trail dust from his clothing. And his legs and lower
back were cramped and sore from long hours spent
pounding his saddle to answer an urgent summons from
Colonel Linton Mackenzie, Commanding Officer at
Fort Bowman.

Fargo had lately been employed as a hunter and scout
for a surveying team in the Nebraska Territory when a
dispatch rider from the fort caught up with him. Mac-

kenzie's urgency forced Fargo to a pace that had been grueling for man and horse, and they both needed this respite before finishing the last leg south toward the Arkansas River.

Again the Ovaro whinnied—still his soft sound of welcome. Fargo suddenly felt more irritated than alarmed. A whicker would send him up the bank and into the pines, weapons to hand. But a low whinny left him reluctant to move right now—the Ovaro was a reliable bellwether of true danger.

You haven't stayed alive all these years, an inner voice nettled him, *by assuming the best.*

Fargo swore softly, trusting his stallion and lulled by the peace and serenity of this spot. His face was tanned hickory nut brown above the darker brown of his close-cropped beard. Despite his relaxed state, eyes the pure blue of a mountain lake stayed in constant motion, for unscouted country was the most dangerous. The surrounding slopes were covered with lush green grass, flax, and bright bluebonnets, and the trees were swollen with new sap and budding into leaf.

Now and then his gaze flicked down to the silvery flash-and-dart of minnows all around him. Their swirling patterns lulled the exhausted man, but when the Ovaro whinnied a third time, the sound prodded Fargo quickly to his feet.

You waited too damn long, that survival voice chastised him.

Fargo agreed. He was screened from view by a tall stand of cattails on the opposite bank. Leaving his boots, Arkansas toothpick, and brass-framed Henry rifle where he'd left them on the bank behind him, he shucked his Colt from its holster and waded through the creek.

Fargo slipped around the cattails and up the opposite bank, studying the clutch of trees hiding the Ovaro. Astounded, he glimpsed the back of a man standing beside the Ovaro as he rifled through a saddlebag. Fargo thumb-cocked his single-action revolver and moved closer on cat feet, puzzled at his vigilant stallion's tolerance of a stranger.

"Stand easy, boy," the thief said softly into the Ovaro's ear, scratching his withers. "That's it. Just stand easy."

Fargo's curiosity deepened when he realized the intruder was ignoring everything else in the saddle pocket to gaze in wonder at an old envelope. And then it came to Fargo: He knew of only one man who could walk up on the Ovaro . . . a man who could not read but greatly valued discarded envelopes, believing there was strange, potent medicine in white man's calligraphy.

"So, Cranky Man, you still think white man's writing is big magic?"

At the sound of a voice behind him, the intruder leaped like a butt-shot dog. His right hand shot up toward the sheath Fargo knew he wore under the collar of his shirt, behind his neck, producing a bone-handle knife with a blade of shiny black obsidian.

Fargo's Colt bucked in his fist, and Cranky Man's greasy flap hat revolved a half turn on his head. He adjusted it with his free hand.

"Put the knife down and turn around slow," Fargo ordered in a voice that brooked no defiance, "or my next shot will send you to your ancestors."

Cranky Man complied, dropping his knife and turning carefully around to face a grinning Fargo.

"Skye Fargo, you son of thunder! Is it really you?"

"It sure's hell ain't the butter-and-egg man," Fargo said, leathering his shooter.

"Well, punch me in the mug and call me pucker face! I *thought* I recognized that fine stallion."

"Hell, you ought to. The first time we met, you were up to the same foolishness—stealing old envelopes from my saddlebags."

"A bad penny always turns up, eh, Fargo?"

"Bad? Old son, you're corroded. But you saved my life once from border ruffians, and once is enough to make you my friend for life."

The heavy-set, half-blood Choctaw Indian had evidently fallen on hard times since Fargo last saw him. Beggar lice leaped from his clothing, and the weathered grooves of his face aged him beyond his years. He wore torn, beaded moccasins, fringed leggings, and a ratty and torn deerskin shirt adorned with beadwork. Brightly colored magic pebbles depended on a string around his neck.

"Where's your horse?" Fargo asked.

"Tethered in the trees nearby."

"So you jumped the rez again, huh?"

Cranky Man flashed his trademark mirthless grin. "Ain't much of a jump—border's only ten miles west of us. I ain't been back there in three months."

"Why?"

"The tormentin' itch, Fargo, the tormentin' itch. Same thing that drives you. Every now and then a man needs a fresh deck—you said so yourself."

"Horse feathers. I recall that cave of yours over near Lead Hill, filled with heisted property. Fresh deck, my ass. You're on the dodge."

Cranky Man resorted to a poker face. "Well, now and then a man also needs to take the geographic cure. It'll blow over—I didn't kill a white man or anything like that. What about you—the hell you doing back in Arkansas?"

"I got a message from Colonel Mackenzie, the commander at Fort Bowman. Asked me to get here quick as I could."

"What's on the spit?"

"That's got me treed. I been out in Nebraska Territory. Ain't seen a newspaper in months. But if they sent for me, it'll be lowdown, dangerous work a sane man wouldn't take."

"Knowing you, maybe it involves an officer's wife, uh?"

The Choctaw was just being his usual, cynical self. But the remark set Fargo back on his bare heels. "Damn, I never considered that, old son. I *did* have a little fun with a captain's wife last time I was there. Maybe there's a firing squad waiting for me."

Cranky Man howled with mirth. "Serve you right. You never did learn to keep it in your pants."

"And you never learned to put a stopper on your gob."

Cranky Man pulled out his hip flask. "Sheer deviltry makes me this way. Spot of the giant killer?"

Fargo waved it off. "I see you're still chummy with the giggle water."

Cranky Man took a belt and capped the flask. Now his face turned solemn. "My medicine has gone bad, Fargo."

"You're so full of shit your feet are sliding. The only bad medicine you got is that Indian burner in your hand—that poison will ruin you. And if you stick around here much longer, you'll be picking lead out of your sitter."

"I like it here. This is nice country."

"It's pretty," Fargo agreed. "But it ain't Fiddler's Green, you reckless fool. You got the Pukes pouring in from Missouri, Jayhawker gangs from up north in Kansas, and warpath braves from the Indian Territory."

"Like I said, I like it here."

Fargo shook his head. "Well, I might need a man to ride with me on this new job. Interested?"

"I'll face danger, for money, but I refuse to work."

"You ugly red son," Fargo said fondly. "You're lazy as the dickens, but I know you're a good fighter. Fetch your horse."

Cranky Man headed into a thicket of trees while Fargo went back for his boots and the rest of his weapons. Then he returned to his Ovaro and quickly checked girth, bridle, and stirrups before he forked leather. Cranky Man emerged from the trees riding his Indian pony, a dish-faced skewbald wearing a flat, stuffed buffalo-hide saddle.

"Where'd you steal that?" Fargo asked, pointing to

the New Haven Arms repeating rifle lashed to Cranky Man's saddle.

"From a white man like you who asked too many questions. I'm all right with a long gun out to fifty or sixty yards, but I don't bother to carry a six-gun—I can kill every time with my knife out to handgun range."

"I wouldn't be here if you couldn't. Let's point our bridles south."

The two men emerged from the growth near the creek into an expanse of rugged hills cut with draws and teeming with sweet clover. A china blue sky showed only a few ragged tatters of cloud, and blackbirds and red-tailed hawks wheeled overhead, wary of these human intruders.

"Yessir," Cranky Man said when they were only fairly started, "this is damn nice country. Peaceful, too."

Just then the Ovaro raised his head, ears pricked, nose quivering.

"Peaceful, huh?" Fargo said.

"For a fact."

"Then you don't know a fact from a hole in your head," Fargo gainsaid. "A graveyard is peaceful, too— we're headed into trouble."

"A life of danger has turned you into a nervous Nellie," Cranky Man scoffed. "This corner of Ark—"

He swallowed the rest of his sentence when a flurry of gunshots, distant but amplified by the hilly terrain, cut him off.

"Let's rustle!" Fargo said, tugging rein and gigging the Ovaro toward the crown of the highest nearby hill even as he speared his brass binoculars from a saddlebag.

A fierce gun battle developed out of sight as both riders climbed the hill. Fargo reached the top first and spotted trouble about two miles below him along bottom country of the Arkansas River. He raised the glasses for a better look as Cranky Man reined in beside him.

"What's wrong?" the Choctaw demanded. "My eyes ain't no good at long distances."

"U.S. Army pay-wagon heist," Fargo said, adding in

a grim tone: "It's a bloody business, and the gang are damn good at what they're doing."

The five bandits had excellent repeating rifles and probably used nearby brushy knolls to gain the element of surprise. The wheel horse hung in the traces mortally wounded and stopping the conveyance. Two of the four soldiers riding guard had managed to unlimber and shoot back, but with the other two, and the civilian shotgun messenger already dead, it was too late to turn the battle.

"They're out of range of your Henry," Cranky Man said.

Fargo nodded, his lips tightly compressed. "They wouldn't even hear it. No point in charging them, either. We'd be two rifles against five, and you can't score hits at this distance—those mange pots can shoot. Besides, it's almost too late now."

Even as Fargo said this, a plume of blood erupted from the driver's head and he tumbled off the box of the coach. One of the two remaining soldiers twisted in his saddle, wounded. Armed only with five-shot Spencers, the two beleaguered troopers made the right call and pounded their horses south across the flats toward Fort Bowman.

"Looks like four men are gone-up cases," Fargo told Cranky Man. "The fire was so heavy the two soldiers couldn't even reload. Now two of the gang are breaking into the payroll box with a chisel and a sledgehammer. The others are going after the telegraph wire on the stage road."

Cranky Man said, "Yeah, but I thought soldier blue gets paid in—whatchacallit?"

"U.S. script instead of gold or federal notes. They do. Only soldiers are allowed to spend it."

"Then why do these jaspers want it so bad?"

Fargo kept his glasses leveled on the scene below as he replied. "It's still backed by gold and can be sold in lots, usually for half its face value, to crooked fort sutlers and other merchants who deal with soldiers. They can exchange it for gold and make a fifty percent profit."

Excerpt from BACKWOODS BRAWL

"What's fifty percent mean?" Cranky Man asked.

"I'll tell you later," Fargo said, intent on learning every detail he could about the human vultures below. The apparent leader wore flaring leather chaps and a red bandanna over the lower half of his face. The upper half was all in shadow under a wide-brimmed hat pulled low. He rode a blaze-faced sorrel and sat a Texas saddle with a high cantle and horn.

Fargo shifted his glasses to the two men destroying the wire.

"Damn," he said with grudging admiration, "this bunch knows 'B' from a banjo when it comes to crime. One has cut the wire between two poles, but they're not stopping there. He wrapped the end of the wire around his partner's saddle horn, and now his partner's riding way off into the distance, pulling down wire with him. A single cut can be repaired in no time. But this way they'll be days stringing new wire."

"It'll be put on the red man," Cranky Man said, "even though Indians won't touch the singing wires for fear of whiteskin big medicine."

"Not if those soldiers make it back," Fargo said. He watched the blue-green glass insulators pop off the poles like buttons on a fat man's vest as the rider galloped off.

"Now they're all leaving," he said finally. "Riding full chisel off in different directions to confuse trackers. C'mon, old son—let's ride down."

Both riders cantered their horses down the face of the hill and onto the sandy flatland. Fargo knew there was no point in pushing his played-out horse: the gang had tossed finishing shots into the heads of all four men, and even the horses had been killed.

"I don't cry over white men killing white men," Cranky Man said. "But these bastards are just downright evil. They coulda took that soldier money without killing everybody. The hell ever happened to 'throw down your guns'?"

166

Excerpt from BACKWOODS BRAWL

At the scene of the crime, Fargo and Cranky Man put the bodies inside the coach to keep the carrion birds off. Cranky Man was clearly agitated, and Fargo knew it was because of his belief that the soul of a recently killed man could leap into another body.

"Your magic pebbles will protect you," he reminded his friend. "The two men who escaped will send a burial detail back."

Fargo gazed around them, his features etched hard as granite. "Their tracks are clear and we could follow one of these trails. But my Ovaro has been sore-used these last ten days, and he's got a loose shoe—I won't risk laming him. Besides all that, I got orders to report to Colonel Mackenzie. Let's take a quick squint around, then dust our hocks south."

Fargo squatted onto his heels and studied the tracks. Usually, in a group of five iron-shod horses, he could find one wearing a flawed shoe. But as if by careful design, all the prints were uniform and unblemished.

"Here's something a mite queer," he finally said. "One of these skunk-bitten coyotes rides a mare."

"How can you tell that from prints?" Cranky Man asked.

"See here where she stood still and pissed behind her legs? A gelding or a stallion couldn't do that."

Fargo was puzzled. Indians would ride a mare, and they were accepted in the land-settled east. But in the rugged West, the bias against them was strong, at least among white men. He stood up.

"Well, the day's still a pup. Let's ride into the fort, and I'll give my report on this."

"I'm damn glad," Cranky Man said, "that we didn't tangle with this bunch."

Fargo grinned wickedly as he swung up into leather. "I wouldn't tack up any bunting just yet, hoss. I got a gut hunch now that I know why Mackenzie sent for me. And that same hunch tells me we *will* be tangling with this bunch."

No other series packs this much heat!

THE TRAILSMAN

Follow the trail of Penguin's Action Westerns at
penguin.com/actionwesterns